Stacey gazed at the man who'd changed her life so much without realizing any of it, and felt comfortable with him.

As a thread of heat wound through her, she had to admit to another feeling—desire. Nothing had changed in that respect. The softening of her stomach, the tightness at her center, the thumping in her chest—all the same. How could she feel like that about a man she'd made love to three years ago and not seen or heard from since? Easily, apparently, if the way he made her feel special was an indicator. Did this mean there was more to her feelings than was logical? But it seemed love wasn't logical and could come out of the blue and bang a person over the head like a thunderclap.

"Anastasia? There was something else you said to me that night."

She stared at him, hope flickering behind her ribs, her tongue moistening her lips. Did he mean what she thought? What if she uttered those words and got it completely wrong? What was there to lose? Her pride could take a knock. "Kiss me, please?"

Dear Reader,

I've only been to London once, and then only for a week. Nowhere near long enough, as it is a fabulous city.

Stacey (short for Anastasia) and Noah met there for one hot night at a hospital dance, and that should've been the end of it. But it wasn't. Stacey spent the next three years trying to track down Noah, with no success. Nor did Noah have any luck finding the woman who filled his dreams at night.

Then three years later, the new surgeon on Stacey's ward is none other than Noah. All the excitement and longing that had been there that first night is still apparent, but now she has to tell him about their daughter. How will Noah cope with this news? Realizing how little she really knows about him knocks her sideways, but she has to trust her gut reaction and tell him.

Life throws curveballs for all of us. I enjoyed straightening this one for Noah and Stacey, and hope you enjoy reading the story as much.

Cheers,
Sue MacKay

suemackayauthor@gmail.com
www.SueMacKay.co.nz

THE NURSE'S SECRET

SUE MacKAY

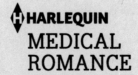

MEDICAL
ROMANCE

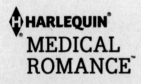

HARLEQUIN®
MEDICAL
ROMANCE™

Recycling programs
for this product may
not exist in your area.

ISBN-13: 978-1-335-14964-0

The Nurse's Secret

Copyright © 2020 by Sue MacKay

This edition published by arrangement with Harlequin Books S.A.

For questions and comments about the quality of this book,
please contact us at CustomerService@Harlequin.com.

Harlequin Enterprises ULC
22 Adelaide St. West, 40th Floor
Toronto, Ontario M5H 4E3, Canada
www.Harlequin.com

Printed in U.S.A.

Sue MacKay lives with her husband in New Zealand's beautiful Marlborough Sounds, with the water on her doorstep and the birds and the trees at her back door. It is the perfect setting to indulge her passions of entertaining friends by cooking them sumptuous meals, drinking fabulous wine, going for hill walks or kayaking around the bay—and, of course, writing stories.

Books by Sue MacKay

Harlequin Medical Romance

London Hospital Midwives

A Fling to Steal Her Heart

SOS Docs

Redeeming Her Brooding Surgeon

Baby Miracle in the ER
Surprise Twins for the Surgeon
ER Doc's Forever Gift
The Italian Surgeon's Secret Baby
Take a Chance on the Single Dad
The Nurse's Twin Surprise
Reclaiming Her Army Doc Husband

Visit the Author Profile page
at Harlequin.com for more titles.

This one is for my editor, Julia Williams.
Her patience and insight have been a lifesaver
at times this past year. Thanks very much, Julia.

PROLOGUE

'LEAVE YOUR BROKEN heart at home and go and do what you're good at and used to enjoy more than anything. Dance the night away. Have some fun, sweetheart.'

Her dad had had a point, Stacey Wainwright admitted as she gazed at the heaving dance floor in front of her. It seemed as though all the medical staff from the London General Hospital were here at the Doctors and Nurses Ball—except of course that wasn't possible, with some having to cover the night shifts.

Since she'd never worked there she wasn't known here, except by the two friends she'd come with, both nurses, but she could still enjoy herself. *If* she let go of the handbrake that had been holding her back over the past year.

It was twelve months since the day she'd been stood up—not at the altar but in her parents' lounge, where she'd been putting the finishing touches to her wedding dress for the big event in four days' time. Her heart hadn't recovered, and neither was it likely to start without her making an effort to get out and do the things she'd used to love.

It didn't come easily since, for the first time ever, she had to do all those things, like dancing, *alone*. So she hadn't bothered.

'Let's rock and roll!' Ada all but leapt onto the dance floor in the beautifully decorated hotel conference room. 'You coming, Stacey?' she asked, with a warning that she'd better be.

It was time to get out and about, Ada had said when mentally twisting Stacey's arm up her back last week to convince her to join them here.

'In a minute.' She needed to get a little more of her delicious cocktail on board to build up the Dutch courage needed for her to let loose. Once she'd loved nothing better than a good party, but nowadays she was out of practice.

Watching her friends making moves nearly in time to the music, without any hesitation, she chuckled. 'Here I was, worrying I wouldn't be able to keep up, but I'll be fine.'

'You into dancing? As in really into it? I've got two left feet, but what the heck? I enjoy myself anyway.' Katie grinned as she poked her cheek with her straw.

She'd only met Katie an hour ago and liked her already. 'I used to do a lot of it.'

Stacey sighed. She'd better get started on having this fun and letting her hair down. Show some resilience. If any man wanted more than a dance or a drink with her, she'd cope. Just say no. She'd only known one man completely, and they'd been best friends most of their lives before their friendship had turned to love. And then Angus had said he didn't want her any more, didn't love her as much as he'd thought, and felt she was still a friend, though no longer the love of his life. He'd snapped his fingers and broken her heart.

Stop thinking about him. He doesn't belong here.

'Is there a dance every year?'

'I think so. I came last year soon after I began working at London General. It was a masked dance party, but the masks didn't last long. I remember two absolutely hammered registrars removed more than their face attire. They weren't exactly studs.' Katie laughed.

'It's usually the ones who aren't who put it all out there.'

'True. You got a man in your life?'

'Afraid not.' If she had he'd be here with her, wouldn't he? Then again, she couldn't guarantee that any more. The man she'd loved with all her being hadn't been there for their wedding. 'I'm taking some solo time at the moment.'

Katie glanced at her with shared sympathy in her eyes. 'You and me both. Don't know why a good man is so hard to find. Or I'm very picky. My last one was a hunk but had the attention span of a gnat when it came to our relationship.'

'I'm sorry to hear that,' Stacey said.

'It's all right. I'm better off without him, though I could do with a replacement soon. What happened with you and your last man?'

Only man. 'We had different ideas about the future.' He'd wanted to spend it with a woman he'd met four weeks before the wedding. After another deep swallow of her drink, Stacey stood up. 'Come on. Let's join the others.' Before the questions became too intense, before she let the past interfere with the present. This was not the night for spilling to someone she barely knew how her one and only boyfriend had had a change of heart.

'About time, you two,' Ada shouted above the music. 'This is fantastic.'

Stacey felt the music grip her, and instantly her feet were moving in time as though they had a mind of their own. Her hips swayed as she raised her arms and went with the rhythm. Closing her eyes, she let the liberating sensations brought on by the music take over. Should've done this ages ago. It *was* fun. *And* relaxing. Surrounded by people intent on having a great night, she was finally having a blast.

Opening her eyes, she stared around at the sea of bodies crowding the floor, all the females glammed up in chic dresses. Her blue and green long strapless dress was complemented by blue nearly sheer leggings and a green bow in her long hair and had all come from the charity shop, the price tag being the decider on what she'd wear. It didn't look half-bad, and the amazing make-up job her friend had done made her feel awesome for the first time in a year. Made her feel light-hearted and free of the past—if only for a few hours.

'Can I have the pleasure?' A deep-voiced, stunning-looking man stood before her.

She smiled. 'Sure, as long as you're not expecting anything too boring.'

'After watching you, I can't imagine you being boring.' Reaching for her hand, he led her deeper into the pulsating crowd.

He'd been watching her dance? She scoped the man before her. His white open-necked shirt was a perfect fit, a tantalising V giving a hint of a broad chest, while his tailored navy-blue trousers enhanced slim hips. Quite the picture, Stacey thought, swallowing hard. He had a strong jawline and an alluring mouth, those full lips giving her ideas she hadn't had in a long time. His eyes, direct and amused, were intriguing, like there was a load of sensuality shining out at *her*. Talk about itemising a guy, but, yeah, she sighed, she liked what she saw. Wanted to know more about him. Was this what waking up was all about? Like a sudden bang on the head? Or was she overreacting as a consequence of only ever dating Angus? If this was what having fun meant she might need to go carefully, not leap in and make a disastrous mistake.

Or I could try relaxing and having that fun I intended when I left home.

Relaxing came easily when she absorbed the music. Her hips swayed, her feet doing their own thing with no worries about being in time. Dancing was in her blood, something she'd done from the day she'd put on the pretty pink dancing shoes Santa had given her when she'd been three. Looking up into the eyes of her partner, she gasped. He was watching her with a smile and warmth in his gaze. Her stomach tightened, and she tripped.

Instantly he caught her, held her long enough for her to get her balance, then dropped his hand.

'Th-thanks.' A gentleman, and gorgeous. Glancing around at the other men on the dance floor, she had to acknowledge he wasn't the only good-looking guy in the room. But…deep breath…he pushed some of her buttons when no one else did or had. Again, she was probably overreacting. *Relax.* Strange how quickly the tension slipped away, and her body continued moving effortlessly in time to the music.

'Come on.' Reaching for her hand, he raised their arms high and with his other hand on her waist, he gently pushed her into a twirl. Next she was being tipped backwards so her hair fell in a long line towards the floor. She spun upright and did another twirl, coming back to face him. 'I'm enjoying this.'

Suddenly Stacey laughed, letting the music and her partner take her on a ride of sensual movement. At least it seemed sensual to her. Another glance at her partner and her breath stuttered in her lungs. He looked as relaxed as she felt. He also looked a little bit surprised. Was he not used to having fun with a stranger, either?

That beautiful mouth spread into a crooked grin. Which set her heart racing.

'You're done this before,' he said.

'Once or twice.' Why *had* she stopped? She didn't need Angus to go dancing. There were plenty of nightclubs near where she lived with her family, and plenty of friends to go with. As of now there must not be any backing out when someone suggested a night on the town. She couldn't use her family commitments as an excuse since her father was over his depression from losing a foot and well on track with studying for an accounting degree. 'I've danced most of my life in one style or another.'

'But nothing boring.' His grin widened.

'You're on to it. You're not so bad yourself.' Flirting? Wow, old Stacey was returning in a rush. No, she hadn't flirted before, never had the need. Angus had always been there like an extra limb.

'Glad you noticed.'

How could she not? Those long, muscular legs moved slickly in time to the music. His hand when he held hers was strong and warm. And made her palm hot and tingly with a sensation she'd long given up on ever feeling again. Except this seemed sharper, more tingly. Guess when a drought broke the ensuing result would feel stronger.

The guy had her hand again, and his other hand splayed on her lower back pressed gently for her to twirl. Once more she was tipped back, then pulled upright and spun around, first one way, then the other.

'That's awesome.' A smile broke across her face as she studied the man holding her. Not once had she felt awkward or worried about taking a tumble. He knew what he was doing and held her just right. He knew what he was doing? What was he doing, apart from dancing with her? Seducing her? If he was, she didn't care. This was why she was here, to enjoy herself, and if things got out of line she would walk back to the table and have another drink before re-joining Ada and co on the dance floor.

The music halted. The sudden quiet was awful. She wasn't ready to stop. Stacey stepped closer to her partner, not wanting him to disappear on her just yet.

A member of the band stood up with a microphone. 'I know this is different to what we've been playing, but it can be fun, if not hilarious. You're such a boisterous crowd that we're going to play a Cha-Cha. Even if you don't know how to deal with that, just leap around in time to the music and you'll be fine.'

Stacey grinned. 'I can Cha-cha. I even quite like it.'

'Me, too,' murmured her dance partner. 'We're good to go.'

Locking her eyes on him, she tried to banish her surprise. He was staying around for more dances with her? Why wouldn't he? She hadn't squashed his toes or made a fool of herself. This was what being single at a party was all about. Getting amongst it, with a good-looking man to boot—who did delicious things to her insides. Perhaps she should look for a duller partner before she lost all common sense. Brilliant idea, if she wasn't intent on at last getting over Angus, and now she was having so much fun moving on, it was suddenly imperative to keep going. The time had come to stop looking back and asking, 'What if?'. This man was hot and fun, so she needed to make the most of him and step outside her comfort zone, which frankly had got boring. 'We are?'

'Yes, unless you've got other plans?'

More laughter bubbled up her throat and across her tongue, obliterating her hesitation. 'Nope, none at all other than enjoying myself.'

'Then bring it on.'

The crowd on the floor was thinning as the band struck up. 'Hope we're not the only ones left out here,' she said.

'We'll give them a show if we are.' Her partner laughed. 'Just relax and follow my lead.'

Taking his hand, she breathed deeply and smelt excitement in the air. And tripped before they'd gone more than two steps. 'Damn,' she muttered. 'That won't happen again.' Concentrate on dancing, not sniffing his scent. Or feeling that warm hand holding hers. Or the way his leg pushed against hers as they raised their legs in unison. The more she immersed herself in the heat surrounding them the more she forgot to focus on where to put her feet, and the better their dancing became.

'You're a natural.' The man's mouth was close to her ear.

Her mouth dried. Settle, girl. He only meant dancing, nothing else. 'Sure am.' She leaned back to look at him. Everything about him was magnificent, wonderful. Abruptly she turned her head, afraid her face was giving too much away.

He spun her around in a circle as they danced. 'What's your name?'

So he wasn't about to stop dancing and say thanks, it's been a pleasure, and walk off the floor. 'Anastasia.' She gave her full name, something she usually only did when filling in legal documentation. About to retract it and say the shortened version, she hesitated.

'It suits you.'

Anastasia it was, then. 'How does a name suit a person?'

'You're fun and happy, as is your name.'

Okay, everyone, listen up. As of now my name is Anastasia, not Stacey.

But she couldn't help being honest. 'I'm not always fun and happy.' Silly woman. Should've kept that to herself.

'No?' Disappointment blinked out at her from

those mesmerising eyes, but his lips quirked as though he was holding back a laugh. 'Guess that makes you normal, then.'

'Afraid so.'

Take that however you wish.

Surely he'd be going in search of someone else to dance with now? Hopefully not when she'd made up her mind to let loose a little— with him. Damn, but she was hopeless at this. Should she grab his hand tightly so he couldn't get away? Yeah, right. Then he'd really be running. So what happened next? More dancing? A drink? Mix and mingle? Talk about being out of practice. 'What are you known by?'

'Noah.'

Odd that they only exchanged first names, but it might be best. All fun, and no tomorrow. Who needed to get caught up in too much talk and a lot less fun? Not her, not tonight. Her pulse rate dipped. What if she wanted to see him again? Getting ahead of herself? Sure she was. Enjoying the moment, finding her feet in this dating game, and *having some fun* was the only way to go. She was fizzing on the inside as the beat in her wrists sped up again. Getting on with the dancing and fun and stop thinking beyond now took over.

Stacey's feet moved, her body swayed, and they were away, her hand in her partner's as they swung their legs high, then he had her in his arms, tipping her back further than before, and she was raising her leg beyond high. Around them others were trying to do the same with mixed levels of success, and some on the sidelines were clapping. At them? Who knew? She wasn't stopping to find out. This was amazing. She could do it all night. She grinned at her partner and continued dancing, rolling her hips and lifting her feet.

When the band finally stopped for a break, Stacey's lungs were working overtime, making her chest rise and fall rapidly. 'I need a drink after that,' she managed between sharp breaths. So much for dancing like a mad thing all night. She was whacked, and thrilled at letting go all the restraints she'd known for the past year. Why hadn't she done this sooner?

'What would you like?' Noah asked, also gasping.

'A mojito, please, Noah.' It did make a difference, knowing his name. They were no longer complete strangers.

'Come on, let's get to the bar before I pass out from lack of liquid.' He took her elbow and led her through the crowd as the DJ put on a song, this one a little quieter and slower. At the bar, he pulled out a stool and continued holding her elbow until she was seated.

Once their drinks were in front of them Stacey thought everything would become awkward. They didn't know each other. Forget awkward, she decided. 'I haven't had so much fun in a long time,' she told him honestly.

'I'd have thought you went dancing every Friday night the way you handled that.'

'Been busy with other things,' she said, adjusting the truth a little, then hurried to change the subject away from her. 'What about you? Do a lot of nightclubbing?'

'Can't say I do. Like you, it's finding the time.'

'Which...' She stopped. No, don't spoil the night getting to know personal details. The anonymity of it all gave her the freedom of being herself, being able to dance and have a drink and not think about overstepping the mark. Of finding who she really was now she was unattached. There might be a totally different person lurking inside, a stronger, more entertaining woman—one who was thinking too much when she should be focusing on now.

'No questions?' he asked with a smile. 'That's a good idea. We're having a great time with no comebacks. Shall we take our drinks out into the foyer? It might be a little cooler there. And quieter.' He spoke close to her ear.

She stifled a gasp as his breath grazed her

skin, sending a ripple of heat to places that hadn't been warm for a long time. When she nodded, he took her elbow to help her off the stool. Definitely a gentleman as well as a hunk. Would she bump into him around the hospital she worked at over the coming days? What would his reaction to her be then? Or hers to him in the light of day and work? There'd been no sign of him during the previous two weeks, or she'd passed him and not noticed his looks. Huh? How likely was that when they instantly turned her into a hot mess?

Relax...go with the fun aspect. He's not hurting you, quite the opposite.

With her glass in one hand, she let him lead her out of the room. This was the way to having a great time.

'Forget quieter.' Stacey laughed, and she was doing a lot of that tonight. The band had come on again, now even louder, and more people were making their way out here. Sipping her drink, she looked around, a big smile on her face. What a night. She wanted to pinch herself.

They stood in companionable silence, cooling down as their drinks disappeared—probably too quickly for someone out of practice, but, hey, she was getting back on her feet, right? Then Noah took her in his arms and began dancing around the edge of the foyer, easily avoiding those standing in groups, talking. As he reached a far corner he paused and gazed down into her eyes. Forget companionable. Butterflies flapped wildly in her stomach. Her skin heated.

'Thank you for a wonderful evening.'

Stacey blinked. 'No, thank *you*.' The heat in her body began dissipating. Was this the end? He'd go one way, she the other? She wasn't ready to say goodnight.

'Thank us. I was dragged here by a friend who I haven't seen most of the night. I'd intended sneaking away early, then along came this amazing dancing lady.'

Phew. That sounded positive, didn't it? 'Is that a chat-up line?' she gasped, unable to believe she'd asked that.

The corner of his mouth lifted as he smiled. 'It wasn't meant to be.'

Damn. If ever the moment to continue moving on from the past was going to happen, surely this was it? Another deep breath. Give it a go. What was there to lose? 'Do you think you could kiss me?'

'Are you a mind-reader?' He bent his head and brushed his mouth across hers.

'Absolutely.' See? It wasn't so difficult to take the enjoyment another step. She inhaled, smelt spice, and man. Oh, yes, man. This man. Hot, strong, pulse-racing scent. Her mouth opened under his, and somehow her breasts were up against his chest and her feet lifting onto their toes. And she was kissing him back. Kissing Noah, a man she'd only met hours ago. And loving it. Loving the sensations zapping through her body, touching her stomach, her toes, her breasts, her centre. All on a kiss.

Splayed hands rested on her hips. Then that delicious mouth pulled back. Serious grey eyes filled with sparks of heat locked on her. Desire? For her? 'Anastasia?'

She nodded slowly. 'Noah.'

'I've got a room upstairs.' He grimaced. 'That sounds corny. But I've been here for three nights as I've packed up my house. I'm heading away tomorrow.'

So she could continue to let her hair down, have that fun she craved, and go home knowing she wouldn't bump into him at the hospital and be embarrassed if it didn't work out. She slipped her hand into his before she could overthink what she was doing. To hell with the past and the future. She'd seize the moment and make the most of what was on offer. 'Yes, please.' Ouch. What did someone say in this situation? She'd never faced it before. How naïve could she be? It was definitely time to get out there and learn a thing or two.

The lift was empty and seemed to fly to Noah's floor. Within moments they were inside his room, kissing as though their lives depended on it. Hot strokes from his tongue turned her to jelly. Had her holding on to him tight, pressing her body to his. Made her crave to be taken. Here. Now. His hand slipped between them to cradle her breast, his finger tweaking the peak, sending bolts of desire slicing through her straight to her point of need. 'Noah,' she growled against his mouth.

Lifting her into his arms, he carried her to the turned-down bed and laid her on it. He stood upright to pull his shirt over his head, exposing the broad, muscular chest she'd imagined. Then he was taking off his trousers. His erection burst free of his underwear and Stacey groaned with need. She wanted him, all the way, now.

'Slowly,' Noah murmured against her ear as he lay down and reached for her, removing her clothes tantalisingly slowly. His hands were magic on her hot skin. His tongue a tease as he tasted her neck, shoulder, first one breast, then the other.

She swallowed a scream, pushing her breasts up closer to that source of wonder. Her hands were working his backside, kneading and stroking, kneading, stroking. Then she reached for him, wrapped her fingers around his hot, throbbing need and rubbed him.

'Anastasia. Wait.' He groped in his trouser pocket, removed his wallet and tugged out a condom packet.

Anastasia. It was like another version of herself. A version who wasn't waiting for her past to catch up and move forward, a version who was moving ahead, making the most of what she had and not wishing for what was gone. Touching Noah, his back, those chest muscles rippling under her fingertips, his flat stomach, and beyond.

Then he was above her, touching, bringing her to a climax like no other, and she was bucking under him. Taking him in and losing herself in a wave of desire and longing and heat.

As he joined her in their release she had one sane thought. *I've done it. I'm free.*

When the alarm went off at five thirty in the morning she slipped out of bed before Noah had opened his eyes and ducked into the bathroom for a quick shower. At some stage during the night he'd mentioned having to leave for the airport by six, and she didn't want to hang around, dragging out the last moments with this amazing man.

Dressed, feeling a sight without make-up, she headed through the room to the door, where she paused for one more look at the man who'd

given her so much without realising it. 'Noah?
Thank you.'

He turned from digging clothes out of his
case. 'Whatever for?'

'Helping me get on with my life.'

'You're welcome.' His smile was a gem, and
one she'd take with her throughout whatever
lay ahead.

CHAPTER ONE

Three years later...

'WELCOME BACK TO the madhouse,' Liz said as Stacey Wainwright stepped into the nurses' office on the surgical ward where she was head nurse.

'Thanks for nothing.' It had been hard, packing her lunch and heading out the door, leaving her daughter behind with Dad after two weeks spending time being with Holly, playing, walking in the park, reading stories. 'I'll get over it,' she told the other nurse.

'And that's not this job you're talking about,' Liz answered with sympathy in her eyes. 'I don't know how you do it.'

Neither did Stacey sometimes. If it weren't for her parents, especially her father, being the daytime carers she'd probably have found some other way to stay solvent and be with Holly, but it wouldn't have been easy. 'I manage. So does Holly. She adores her granddad.'

'Who spoils her rotten.'

'Funny, that. He never spoilt me or Toby.' Her brother took pleasure in teasing Holly about that, even when she was too young to understand.

'Grandparents' rights, eh?' Liz tapped the computer screen. 'Let's get this done so I can go get some breakfast before sleeping the day away. It was hectic in here last night. Two new admissions, both with post-trauma surgery after a multiple pile-up in the Rotherhithe Tunnel. I've got individual care on each, but they shouldn't deteriorate unless the unexpected happens, which we know often does.'

Liz continued going through the patient list. 'This one.' She pointed to the last name on the list. 'Jonathon Black. Keep an eye on him. He had his pancreas removed thirty-six hours ago because of cancer. Early this morning he complained of increased pain and his temperature's spiking. Joel upped his antibiotics in case there's an infection developing.'

Stacey studied the notes on the screen. 'Joel wasn't too concerned?' If the duty registrar was okay with these results then so should she be, yet unease was rising, and she knew not to ignore that.

'He suggested a CBC, but I haven't had time to take blood.'

'I'll see to it.' Nothing like a normal white-cell count to counteract the sense of an out-of-control infection coming into play. 'Anything else I need to know? Apart from who's getting married, divorced, having another baby?' She grinned. She'd missed everyone while she'd been away. They were a tight-knit group on the ward, and outside work.

'Come on. We were expecting you to come back with some gossip about what you've been up to and who you've been seeing.'

'Get out of here. I'm going to see Mr Black.'

I'm not telling you about the guy I went on a date with.

There'd be no end to the quizzing. Anyway, while she liked Matthew she wasn't overly enamoured and wouldn't be following up. The few times she'd dated over the years since *that* night with Noah in an effort to keep moving on had only made her regret more than ever not getting his contact details.

Not only because of Holly either, but because there was no denying the intense longing to see him again she couldn't douse no matter how hard she tried. He'd got to her in unexpected ways, like being kind and gentle, exciting and sexy. Of course there was a lot to learn about him, and she wanted to more than she could believe, even after all this time.

That one night when she'd danced like she'd never quite done before, or since, had totally distracted her from the past and made her happy beyond belief. It had been out of this world, as had the man she'd danced and made love with.

Talk about a life-changer. Holly was the result, and she wouldn't alter a thing, other than find the man and tell him he was a father. So far, her endless search had come up blank. It was hard with only a first name to go on. The world was full of Noahs, apparently. He'd got away and her disappointment was huge. There'd been a connection she'd not expected, and she wanted to follow up. Sigh.

'Hey, Stacey?' Liz called. 'There's a new surgeon on the ward. He started a week ago, so I haven't met him since I've been on nights and he hasn't been called in. He's Jonathon Black's surgeon. Mr Kennedy. Quite something, apparently. And I'm not talking about him as a surgeon.' She grinned.

Stacey waved a hand over her shoulder. 'Thanks, Liz. I'll give him your phone number when I see him.' A laugh followed her down the ward as she went to see Mr Black.

She'd meet the surgeon soon enough. In the meantime she had a job to do. 'Hello, Jonathon.

I'm Stacey Wainwright, the head nurse on this ward. I've just returned from leave and have been getting up to speed with your details.'

'I heard you were due back today.' His face was red and puffy around eyes filled with pain.

Stepping across to read the monitor showing his BP, heart rhythm and temperature, she said, 'I hear you're uncomfortable and that your temperature has risen. What about pain in the region of your surgery? Has that quietened down since the op?' Despite the notes on the computer, she liked to ask patients about their symptoms, in case any details were left out.

'It's hurting more than ever. The pills I've been given haven't helped.'

'Do you mind showing me where this pain is exactly?' Stacey lifted the sheet to pull up the hospital gown he still wore for ease of access and keeping pressure off the wound a pyjama bottoms waistband might cause.

'All around here.' Without touching his abdomen, he indicated an area forward of where his pancreas would've been situated.

'Not up here?' She lightly touched the surgical wound.

'That hurts, but the deep pain is away from there.'

Add in the thirty-eight-point-five-degree temperature, the deep red shade in his face and upper body, and there was definitely something more than an infection of the internal wound going on. Or so her gut told her. 'I'm going to take a blood sample and send it to the lab. Then I'll call your surgeon and inform him what's going on.' She'd also put Jonathon's breakfast on hold for now. If he had to go back to Theatre he didn't need food in his belly. 'We'll get this sorted for you.'

'Thank you, Nurse. I am worried that something else is happening.'

'Try to relax. I know, easily said. Please don't accept food or anything to drink.'

He nodded. 'I understand.'

'Show me again where it hurts the most.' When he indicated the same spot, where the appendix was, she asked, 'On a score of one to ten, ten being the highest, what would you say the pain is?'

'Eight.'

'Right. I'll get the blood-test kit.' On the way she stopped at the office and asked for Mr Kennedy's speed-dial number. She had a sinking feeling that whatever was causing Jonathon's distress was rapidly becoming urgent.

'Mr Kennedy.'

Her brow furrowed at the sudden voice on the other end of the line. Shaking away an odd sensation she couldn't explain, she said briskly, 'I'm

Stacey Wainwright, head nurse on Surgical. I think you need to see Jonathon Black. He has severe pain and an increased temperature. I'm about to take an EDTA specimen.' She filled in the details.

'It's likely an infection of the wound, possibly internal. I'll be up in a few minutes.'

'Thank you. I have a feeling it's something else. Appendicitis, even peritonitis.'

'I'll investigate all possibilities when I get there.' The phone went dead.

Fair enough. He was the doctor. She the nurse. In the past she'd met doctors who put nurses down, but she'd never been able to keep her thoughts to herself when she believed there was something happening with a patient that hadn't been considered. He hadn't had time to consider anything, hadn't observed his patient this morning, and she was about to meet him. She hoped Mr Kennedy wasn't going to be the kind of doctor to give a rebuke for putting her opinion out there.

She shivered. That sense she'd missed something when he'd first answered her call returned. Like she knew him, but as far as she could recall she hadn't worked with any doctor of that name. Guess she'd know soon enough.

With the blood-test kit in hand, she returned

to her patient. 'Jonathon, let's get this done. Your surgeon will be here to see you shortly.'

'You don't muck around, do you?' His smile was tight with pain but there was also relief in his voice.

'I try not to.' She pushed up the sleeve of the gown and put the tourniquet in place before wiping an area above his vein with antiseptic fluid. 'One sharp scratch.' The needle slid in, and the tube began filling. She decided to take a tube to be spun for serum as well in case the surgeon asked for biochemistry tests. It would save time and discomfort for Jonathon if she didn't have to come back for another sample. 'There, done.' Snapping off the tourniquet, she withdrew the syringe and began labelling the tubes.

'Didn't feel a thing.'

Probably because he was focused on the pain from his abdomen. He looked worse than he had minutes ago. If his appendix was playing up then she'd bet her lunch it was now in an advanced state and would need urgent surgery. Slipping the tubes into a plastic bag, she stood at the end of the bed and said, 'I'll get this taken to the lab, then I'll be back.' Hopefully by then the surgeon would be here, and she could relax.

The door to the room darkened. 'Good morning, Jonathon. I hear you're having more pain than you should be.'

The bag containing the blood sample slid from her fingers onto the bed. The blood in her body dived south, leaving her head dizzy. Her mouth dried. Her stomach roiled. Noah?

Jonathon looked beyond her. 'Mr Kennedy— am I glad to see you. Though Stacey's been very helpful, hasn't doubted that I'm telling the truth about increased pain.'

Mr Kennedy. Phew. She could relax, put her head back on straight, make her stomach behave. It wasn't Noah. Why would he be Noah? The same sensations that had excited her that night three years ago when she had been with him were winding through her, tightening her in places, softening her in others. What were the odds? For one, because he'd been at the hospital ball she'd presumed he worked in the medical world, yet she could've been wrong. And if she'd been right there were numerous hospitals in London, and a darned sight more out in the world. Looking online was an unsolvable nightmare, like asking where was the best place to go for ice cream. She hadn't seen his friend at the ball at all so couldn't track him down, and the hotel Noah had been staying at had refused to give out his name. No, it wasn't Noah. Couldn't be. Though she wanted to find him for Holly's sake. *And mine.* She'd believed she'd be ready if the chance came up. Got that wrong. She was anything but ready.

With a deep breath, she turned around. 'Hello, Mr...'

Noah stood before her. Looking as stunning as last time she'd seen him. More so. Her memories hadn't lied. That good-looking face with the strong jawline and wide mouth was exactly as she recalled. His suit enhanced his broad shoulders and the wide chest that led down to slim hips and muscular thighs. Oh, man, could she remember those. On a deep breath, she looked up into familiar grey eyes. Yes. Deep grey like these ones. The only difference was the shock radiating out at her.

Gripping the bed end to keep from face-planting on the floor, she stared at Noah. Yes, Noah. No one else. The man who'd helped her get on with life by being exciting, and kind, and tender, and fun. The man who'd hung around in her head ever since, teasing her about the feelings she had for someone she'd known for less than a day. Warm feelings of longing that were making themselves known right now. He'd also been a part of what had unexpectedly thrown her into turmoil and given her the greatest gift ever. Holly. Her daughter. *Their* daughter.

Stacey's knees buckled and her ribs hit the

end of the bed. Fighting to stay upright, she held on tight and closed her eyes to focus. It couldn't be him. But it was. Finally she'd found Noah. Ironic, because today she hadn't been looking for him. Worse, he was as attractive as she remembered, which was odd, because she'd never thought she'd feel this way again after Angus had jilted her. *He'd* been the love of her life.

Yet Noah had excited her very differently, had her wondering if her love for Angus had been all she'd thought. Now, three years on, she'd accepted that her one-night fling with Noah was always going to have been more exciting than the man she'd known all her life. She'd tried to move on from Noah and that night. One night was a lot to hang hopes and dreams on, but impossible to forget with Holly a constant reminder.

Then there were those memories of respect and gentleness, of giving herself to him. Here he was, standing a metre away, and she knew she'd been wrong to think she could forget him. He was special. He had pressed all her buttons. Staring at him now, her throat dried even as her knees started tightening to keep her upright. 'Noah,' she squeaked.

He gasped, 'Anastasia?'

Strike me down. Noah stared at the apparition at the end of his patient's bed. After all this time the woman who'd given him one night to remember, to *never* forget, was standing in front of him, looking as stunned as he felt. 'Anastasia? As in Stacey Wainwright?'

Her nod was abrupt. 'Yes. Noah, as in Mr Kennedy, surgeon, I presume.' There was the faintest twitch at one corner of her exquisite mouth.

A mouth he'd kissed deeply and longed for again and again over the years when he'd been so far away from London, at the bottom of the world. A mouth that had done wondrous things to his body. Then he surprised himself by chuckling. They'd talked like that the first and only time they'd been together, each on the same track as the other, like they were kindred souls. There was a thumping going on behind his ribs, as though he was happy to bump into Anastasia again. Which he was, but so happy he felt a new world was opening up before him?

He'd often wondered what had happened to the woman with an easy sense of fun and eyes that sparkled with merriment. The first woman he'd felt anything for since Christine, the ex who'd let him down big time.

He breathed deep. Yes, there it was. That citrus tang hung in the air between them. A scent he'd taken with him as he'd crawled out of bed the next morning and hurriedly prepared to get

to Heathrow and eventually New Zealand in
an attempt to get away from his father's family and have time for himself. He'd joined his
cousin from his mother's side, shared an apart-
ment and worked in the same hospital while getting a wealth of experience in general surgery.

Anastasia had gone with him in his head,
often tempting him to return home and hunt her
down. He hadn't, because he was cautious about
giving his heart to anyone again. Yet deep down
he did want to find a woman to trust his heart
with, to love unconditionally—if only he could
let go of his hang-ups from the past.

He'd dated on and off, and no other woman
had been a patch on this special lady he'd had
so much genuine fun with three years ago. She'd
raised hope he might be able to find the love
he'd spent a lifetime looking for. She'd become
an itch under his skin, a constant irritation. Now
here she was, beautiful, and very real. 'We meet
again.'

Her eyes were wide, and those yellow and
green flecks in the deep brown shade were shining. That thick, dark blonde hair was tied back
in a ponytail falling down her back as straight
as it had been when he'd swung her around on
the dance floor. Her hair had been loose then,
silk running between his fingers. His muscles
tightened at the memory. And another of her

mouth on his skin as she whispered hot, sweet nothings. Now, her voice was cooler, like she was fighting with this sudden reunion. 'We do. And we'd better get on with why we're here.'

His patient. On the phone she'd suggested Jonathon might have appendicitis, and he'd wondered if she was right. For once, he didn't want to be here, looking into a patient's details and making arrangements for whatever was required. No, he wanted to snatch Anastasia—to hell with Stacey—to him, wind his arms around her and hold on tight. He didn't want her to go away. He'd longed to find her, and here she was.

Now what? Walk away while he could? Because something said it would get harder to do the longer he hung around, that if a deeper relationship with Anastasia failed he'd be more heartbroken than when Christine had done her number on him. Anastasia was special, but that didn't mean she'd be good for him. Did he truly want to keep avoiding risking his heart or did he want that love he'd always longed for since his parents had died? Was he going to risk all to find out? How could he not? She'd be almost impossible to walk away from this time, and they'd only just met again.

'Noah?' She leaned close, watching him with a warning in her eyes.

Of course. Forget what *he* wanted. He *was*

at work and Jonathon was waiting for him to gather his scattered brain cells and be of some use. But, hell, after all this time wondering about the woman he'd spent a beautiful night with, he'd bumped into her, and he just couldn't let it go. Not even briefly. 'Talk later over coffee,' he told her, hauling back his shoulders and stepping up to the bed. 'Jonathon, I hear you're suffering more pain than when I saw you yesterday, and that your temperature has risen.'

'Yes, I started feeling the pain around lunchtime yesterday but thought it was all to do with the operation. Only the pain kept increasing, despite the drugs I was given, and now it's unbearable.'

'I'll take a look.' Anastasia had already closed the curtains around them and disappeared just when he needed her as a nurse, and not a wonderful memory. Flicking the curtain aside, he headed for the door, only to pause as she came towards him.

'I've sent a haematology specimen to the lab as ordered by Joel. I also took a biochemistry blood in case you required more tests.'

She was onto it. 'I can't argue with that.' Relieved she hadn't dashed away to put space between them and send in another nurse, he struggled to keep on the subject of Jonathon's problem. 'You think this is more than the original site becoming infected?'

Her eyes widened as she stared at him. Obviously not used to a doctor asking her opinion. 'The pain Jonathon's having is eight out of ten, and where he indicates it's coming from isn't where you operated.'

He had no doubt she had an idea what the problem was. 'Let's take a look.' He turned back into the cramped space around the bed. 'Jonathon, can you show me where this pain is.'

Anastasia helped their patient expose his abdomen, then she stood aside.

Noah tried not to breathe too deeply to avoid that scent that said *Anastasia*, and got on with what he was good at. As his fingers probed Jonathon's abdomen he felt the man tense. 'There? Or here?'

'The second place. The other hurts but when you touch the second one, it's like a knife going in.'

Which was what was probably going to happen soon. 'I'll wait to see what your white-cell count is but I suspect it's going to be high.'

The man looked at him blankly, shaking his head. 'Meaning?'

'White cells fight infections and to do that they rapidly increase in number. Unfortunately, the result will be the same if there's an infection where I removed your pancreas. But going with where the pain is, I believe…' He paused and looked across to Anastasia. 'I think you've got acute appendicitis, which means the appendix has to be removed.'

Her mouth twitched. But she remained silent.

Damn, how he remembered that twitch. It had wound him up so much, had him touching her again and again. He really knew so little about her, but it seemed he knew what mattered. He'd like to change that, add to his memories. True? Yes, damn it, it was.

'More surgery?' Jonathon's shaky question broke the spell.

Concentrate on the patient. 'Yes, Jonathon. I know you won't be keen but there's no choice. If we're right—' Anastasia's eyebrows rose. 'If *we're* right, that appendix has to come out as soon as possible or you'll become dangerously ill.'

'This doesn't have anything to do with the first operation, does it?'

Fortunately not. Noah shook his head. 'The pancreas and appendix are two separate organs. This is a completely new problem, and bad timing. Or you could say good timing because we're onto it, and you don't have to wait for surgery.'

'Whatever. You're the boss.' Jonathon shrank back into his pillow.

Anastasia quickly fixed his robe in place and tucked the bed cover over the worried man. 'You'll be fine. Mr Kennedy did a great job of that pancreas, so this next op will be just as good.'

How did she even begin to know that? A scar told an observer very little, except maybe he could be a tailor if he ever wanted to change careers. Looking at her, she smiled softly at him, and tenderness sneaked into Noah's tense muscles at the thought she'd believe he was a capable surgeon even if until a few minutes ago she hadn't even known what his specialty was.

He liked being accepted in a positive way without having to explain himself, and Stacey had just done that. His shoulders loosened some more. It didn't happen often. In fact, he'd struggled most of his life since he was ten to be good enough at anything, especially where his uncle was concerned.

Apparently he had his mother's genes, and those were wrong for the Kennedy family. His mother had enjoyed life immensely, had been a loving person who'd seen the best in everyone and not the bad. According to Uncle Robert, she'd led his father away from his role in life by being too outgoing and bringing all sorts of people into their circle, instead of toeing the line and behaving properly. When Robert had disapproved of Christine, it had been more of the same complaints, except for once he'd got it right about her being a greedy woman who'd wanted nothing more than Noah's wealth.

Noah glanced at the nurse helping his patient. She had a similar zest for life to his mother. Being proper would definitely be anathema to her, if he'd read her correctly that night. He'd swear he had. 'Can you let me know the moment those lab results come in? And get a CPR on the bio sample.'

'Sure.' A smile lit up her face. 'Where will I find you?'

As in she didn't want to lose him again? Not yet, she couldn't. Not until they'd had a coffee together, at least. He laughed at that idea. Unbelievable, but sitting down with a coffee would be fine. Talking, catching up on the last three years—make that all the years because they knew so little about each other—held an allure that he had to follow up on. And therefore a reason not to spend time together away from this ward, and getting caught up in her loveliness. He downplayed the hidden message he thought might be in her question. 'Call my hospital number. I'll be waiting to hear from you,' he said professionally, trying not to imagine kissing her again.

The smile slipped off that delightful mouth. 'Right.'

He left the room without a backward glance because if he looked back, he'd stay talking when he had a surgical list to get through, one that had been increased with Jonathon Black now needing an appendectomy. Not a doubt. No ignoring that scent that was Anastasia either. Or the way his step was lighter than usual as he made his way down the ward to the lift. At least the citrus didn't follow him. Though memories of a shapely figure, gentle hands, soft skin, incredibly sexy moves on the dance floor, and in that darkened hotel room did.

Anastasia, Stacey, worked here where he'd been contracted as a general surgeon at the same time as picking up a partnership in a private practice along the road. He'd found her, and could admit to certain feelings that he'd been trying to deny. Now that particular riddle was finally solved, he didn't have a clue what to do next. Take a chance? Or back off? So typical in his world of relationships. After Christine he never intended getting caught up in another one—they hurt too much when they fell apart. Yet while his encounter with Anastasia had only involved hours it felt as though a lot more of

him had got caught up with her. He was afraid
to try for love again, even if Anastasia had left
her mark on him. They had seemed to click the
two times they'd been together, like they just
knew each other even when they didn't. Not in
an expansive way yet. He sighed.

The lift pinged and he stepped inside amongst
other staff. Did he really intend staying single
for the rest of his life? Not having a family to
love and cherish like his parents had him until
they'd been abruptly taken? He didn't believe
he was loveable. His relatives hadn't come anywhere close when it came to loving him. They
hadn't loved him at all, and still didn't.

Then there was Christine. He hoped Anastasia was the polar opposite. Not every woman
was a money-hungry ice queen. Christine had
fooled him into thinking otherwise simply because he'd been desperate to find a happy, loving environment like his life had started in. Not
every woman was Christine. She came from a
poor background and had a lifelong dream of
marrying money.

But how did he know Anastasia wouldn't be
the same? She might be just as good at putting
up a façade. Get a grip. At that dance she'd
smiled wholeheartedly at him and made him feel
warm and special. In the morning she'd turned
down his offer of a taxi home. Then again, any-

one with half a brain could've sounded genuine, especially to him after the greatest sex he'd had in a long time.

Ping. He made to step off, hesitated and looked at the floor indicator. Great. He'd gone up rather than down, and the lift had more floors to go before returning to the theatre level. Stepping back, he found a corner and leaned back against the cold wall.

It had been one night in paradise. No questions, no hang-ups, no expectations. He'd been himself, a rare event, resulting in a fantastic time. Since then he'd often wondered who the woman he'd made love to the night of the dance was... Where she worked...if she was a doctor or a nurse...did she work at London General— which, according to his friend when he asked, she didn't—and did she ever think of him?

Now he had the answers to most of those questions, he needed to find out more. The way she'd already tipped him sideways worried the hell out of him. Temptation in a nurse's uniform. If he ever found the love he'd been seeking for so long, would he always be waiting for the axe to fall?

His parents had been the best mum and dad out there, loving him unconditionally, making him feel wanted, needed. He'd loved them back just as much, though naturally he'd pushed every button they'd had and some. He'd had a happy family life—until that fateful night when he'd been ten years old.

He'd been staying with his best friend down the road in Bloomsbury when the doorbell had rung. It had been so loud and shrill in the quiet evening that he'd felt a chill up his back. He'd never been able to explain why he'd known something wasn't right and that it involved him. Uncle Robert had been standing on the doorstep, and the news had been grim.

His parents were dead, killed in a car accident, and from then on he was to live with his uncle and aunt and cousins. It was a lie because within three months he'd been sent to boarding school, and had only gone back to the house for those school holidays when he hadn't gone to his friend's home. Since that day he'd been searching for love like that that had been stolen from him, but he'd always been afraid that if he found it, it would once again be whipped away.

Yet he'd fallen for Christine and married her. In the beginning she'd been friendly, and keen to have two children, though he'd learned after the wedding that making love was only for ovulation days. Oh, and the fortune he'd inherited from his father was necessary to keep her happy, and the London house equally important. It hadn't taken long to realise that the deep, abiding love his parents had had and which he'd been looking for wasn't happening with Christine so he'd filed for divorce. Thanks to the prenup he still had most of his inheritance. Letting his father down on that aspect would've decimated him. But neither had he been miserly, making sure Christine didn't go without.

Ping. 'What floor do you want?' a young woman asked.

'Two, thanks.' Better let her press the button. That way he might arrive where he needed to be.

Not where he wanted to be. Which was in a café with coffees on the table between him and Anastasia. If she even liked coffee. He'd better start calling her Stacey, in front of staff at least. That'd keep everyone else away from trying to guess what their relationship was about. It might also help him remain grounded and not rushing into something he might later regret.

To think he'd woken that morning fully expecting a normal, chaotic day in Theatre and on the ward, dealing with other people's problems, and getting up to speed with the staff and this hospital and how different it was to work in London compared to Auckland, where everyone was more relaxed with each other, and he'd enjoyed getting to know his cousin from his mother's side. It had been tempting to stay but the sense of unfinished business back in London had nagged.

Anastasia had also always popped into his head at those moments, and many others. Already there'd been days he'd regretted returning home, but responsibilities had called in the form of his uncle and aunt, and he wasn't one to neglect duty. Even when it involved people who'd neglected him. So here he was, and he'd make the most of the situation.

His thoughts returned to Anastasia. Her ready smile and sparkling eyes, her deep, genuine laughter full of happiness. Her hourglass figure, and those dance moves.

His gut clenched, his heart flipped, and a sigh trickled over his lips. Should've stayed in Auckland. It would've been easier, safer, and a whole lot more boring now that he'd found Anastasia again.

CHAPTER TWO

STACEY HELPED JONATHON into a clean gown. 'The porter will be here shortly to take you down to Theatre. Mr Kennedy has put you first on his list and is waiting for you.'

He'd prioritised Jonathon when she'd called with the lab results, said he'd already decided he was going to operate because something was seriously wrong, and he believed it was appendicitis. And he'd acknowledged Anastasia's opinion. Yep. They did have an unexplainable link between them.

Just listening to that deep gravelly voice gave her the shivers in the nicest, warmest way possible, and reminded her of what lay ahead before she could even consider anything else. He was the father of her daughter. That would be a game changer. Whether he liked her or not. Whether he wanted to spend time with her, or never see her again other than on the ward.

Another thought stopped her in her tracks.

What if he turned against her when she told him about Holly? Got nasty and said she was lying? All very well being able to prove his parenthood, but that didn't mean he'd remain friendly. She might have to apply for a new position. She loved this job, was so proud of being head nurse, and changing jobs would hurt like hell.

So don't even consider it. Stand your ground. You've done nothing wrong.

'The doc doesn't muck around, does he?' her patient said.

'It appears that way.' Was Noah like that in all his endeavours, or just with patients requiring urgent care? How would he take her news? It'd knock him for sure. But how would he react? She doubted he'd procrastinate. He'd taken her into the centre of the dance floor the moment she'd said yes to dancing with him, and when she'd asked him to kiss her he hadn't hesitated. A man who knew his own mind. Another point in his favour was that he hadn't been pushy or demanding when they'd made love. He'd been considerate and gentle. Yes, and hot and wonderful. She flapped a hand in front of her face. 'It's warm in here.'

'Can't say I'm noticing,' Jonathon commented.

'That's probably nerves. I'll get you a blanket. Oh, hi, Jim. Jonathon, your porter's here.'

Dashing to the storeroom, she got a blanket, and after wrapping Jonathon up snug she went to check on one of the women who'd been involved in the pile-up last night. 'How's she doing, Ada?'

The nurse looking after Patsy Miller was reading the cardiac monitor attached to her patient. 'She nodded off after I administered some morphine. She has a history of arrhythmia and was operated on for a perforated bowel last night. Her obs are good, though I'm watching that heart monitor like a hawk.'

'Good. Let me know if anything changes.' She headed back to the hub to look at the notes on Mrs Miller. Noah was her surgeon, which meant he'd been working during the night, and didn't look at all tired this morning. It also meant another reason for him to possibly visit the ward later. No avoiding him. *I don't want to.* But there was the Holly issue. He had to be told sooner rather than later, or when he heard about Holly, he'd think she'd been holding out on him for her own reasons.

Damn it, she liked the man, or what little she knew of him. Liked? Okay, he'd been fun, caring, sexy as all be it, and prepared to stop what they'd started if she'd had a change of heart. He'd insisted on paying for a taxi for her, though he hadn't won that one. She more than liked him, way more. She froze on the spot. What if he was married? Already had a family of his own? Why hadn't she thought of that before? Because she'd hoped they might have more in common than one night. Not thinking about that until she'd seen him again.

Whatever the answers to her questions, he was Holly's father, and didn't know it. He had to be told. Next move—hers.

She'd do it ASAP. She needed to ask Noah to have that coffee he'd mentioned. Forget time to come to terms with him being back in her life. But though it was all very well knowing and believing in what was the right thing to do, it was a totally different prospect now the time was here to follow through. Keeping Holly a secret had never been on the agenda. Still wasn't. Except she felt awkward about walking up to him and saying, 'Hey, have I got news for you.' So, ask him to meet after work.

'Want a coffee?' Jason leaned over the counter, interrupting her chain of thought.

Not with you, or anyone other than Noah. Deep breath. 'Sure do. I'll be along in a minute.' Stacey glanced at her watch and was surprised to see nearly an hour had passed while she'd been doing the 'paperwork'. Noah would've finished operating on Jonathon Black. Unless there was more to the man's pain than they'd believed.

The phone by her elbow rang. 'Surgical ward, Stacey speaking.'

'Anastasia. Sorry, Stacey, it's Noah. I thought you'd like to know your summation of Black's condition was correct, though it'd gone further and turned into peritonitis.'

Coming from him in that deep, gravelly voice, she liked it when he said 'Anastasia'. He made it sound special, theirs from that wonderful night they'd shared. Except everyone would want to know why he did. She huffed out a breath. 'You got it in time. Are there any side-effects at the pancreatic site?'

'We need to be vigilant over infection. I've prescribed stronger, intravenous antibiotics to start immediately.'

This was good. They were surgeon and nurse, discussing a patient, not two people catching up after a long time with only hot memories—and a child—between them.

Don't forget where this has to go—Holly.

A quiver started up in her hands. 'I'll make sure everyone knows the situation.'

'Anastasia, how do you feel about catching up with me away from here?'

Excited. Nervous. Scared. Happy. No, not happy with Holly in the middle of everything. But it had to be done. *Ta-da, ta-da*, went her heart. Why couldn't her life run smoothly so she could shout, *Yes, I'd love to, and by the way...*

'I'd love to.'

She had to, didn't she? If nothing else, she had to suss him out as her daughter's father. Forewarned was forearmed, or so they said. Just because she found him attractive and desirable, it didn't mean he was perfect. Certainly didn't endorse him as a parent, though even in the short time she'd spent with him she'd swear he'd be a good father. Maybe she was biased. After one night in his bed? Well, his kindness, gentle touches and readiness to follow her lead did say a lot about a man. But there was no delaying telling him the truth.

A low chuckle came through the phone, making her smile. 'You haven't changed a bit.'

Oh, yes, I have. Because of you, I got over Angus. Though I'm still wary of trusting a man with my heart again. Also, because of you, I'm a mum with the most adorable little girl imaginable.

'Call me when you have a spare moment.' The phone banged hard as she put it back on its holder.

Closing her eyes, she pictured Holly on the swing in the park yesterday, giggling as the hem of her pink, frilly skirt blew up under her chin. Holly, her darling girl. Noah had to love her. Had to. No option, or she didn't know what she'd do. As long as he didn't try to take Holly away from her. He wouldn't. But compared to her family, he'd be well off. He was a medical specialist so might think he could provide a better life for their daughter. He'd have the battle of all battles if he tried that on. But she was getting ahead of herself.

He knew nothing about what had gone on in her life after they had parted that morning in his hotel room. She wanted to take her time learning more about his lifestyle and him, before exposing herself and Holly, but she didn't have that right. She could only trust her gut instinct—Noah Kennedy would do the right thing by them all. Fingers crossed.

'I gave up waiting.' Jason plonked a full mug in front of her and pulled out the other seat at the counter.

'Sorry, you know how it is. Mr Black's had an appendectomy and will be back on the ward later this morning. We need to keep a close eye on him for developing infection at the original operation site, and make sure it's not ramping up this latest problem.'

'Poor guy. He'll be sore for a while.' Jason munched on a biscuit. 'So what do you think of our new surgeon?'

My lips are sealed.

'So far I like him.' She spluttered into her coffee. 'He seems to know what he's doing,' she said, trying for a smile but suspecting it came off as a grimace.

'Guess that means he'll be too busy for his ward round today.'

She shook her head. 'No mention of it.' She needed to know if Noah was going to turn up so as not to get taken by surprise and look out of her depth. Ward rounds were a piece of cake, all part of her duty, but Noah suddenly appearing in front of her was not. 'How much have you had to do with him?'

Jason shrugged. 'Much the same as with any of them. He's an okay guy, though. Not arrogant and willingly shows concern for his patients. They all seem to think he's the best.'

He's the best.

That Stacey understood. Jason had described the man she'd met, without the patients. He had been the best for her when it came to dancing and making love. And sharing jokes and laughter. And changing her life. The phone rang again, and she left Jason to deal with the caller. Her work inbox was full of non-urgent messages that had to be dealt with sooner rather than later, because the inward flow never stopped and only caused her a headache if she ignored them. Staying on top of everything was the only way to work in this busy environment that she loved being a part of.

It'd been her ambition to become a nurse since she'd been a child and played with her grandmother's nursing badge. Once she'd even dressed up in a white uniform and cap like Gran used to wear as matron and had gone off to the fancy-dress party at school, proud as punch to sport the treasured badge. That badge had become hers when Gran had died, and was still in her jewellery box, polished and shining.

'Have you got a free moment, Anastasia?'

Her head jerked up and her gaze met Noah's full on. 'Yes, I have.' A glance at the wall clock showed midday. Past lunchtime for her. Where had the morning gone? Out with those blasted emails, no doubt. Rising from her seat, she rubbed her lower back, which was aching from sitting so long hunched over the keyboard when she wasn't talking to various nurses about their patients. 'I hear Jonathon's a lot more comfortable than he was first thing this morning.'

'I'm pleased to hear it. Now, is there somewhere we can talk? I don't have long with Theatre beckoning.'

'Who do you want to see first?'

Noah looked down at her, his mouth doing that one-sided smile thing. 'You.'

'This isn't a ward round?' He was still watching her, and that smile was still happening. Her insides softened. He was gorgeous.

'Not at all.'

Of course he only did those twice a week. 'Oh.'

'Don't tell me you're stumped for words. I don't believe it.' He grinned.

She couldn't help laughing. He had a way of talking to her that made her feel good about herself. 'You'd better.'

'The staff kitchen? It's close and time's short.'

The poky room where they made coffee and ate sandwiches at a speed that gave them indigestion? Her heart dipped. Not much going to happen in there, especially if anyone else was there. There'd be no space to breathe in air. 'Sure.' She led the way, aware of Noah behind her every step.

Despite the tight knots in her neck and shoulders she felt good. Hope fought with the Holly knots in her stomach. If she and Noah could get along this easily after a very brief history then the future could be bright. Not for them as a couple or anything so deep and meaningful, but so they could share parenting. Actually, that made her nervous. She wasn't ready to give up any of what she had with her daughter, while she wanted so much more with Holly's father for herself.

He touched her shoulder lightly. 'Where have you gone?'

She shivered. His touch sent sparks in all directions. Beware. This man saw too much for her liking. 'I'm right here, ready to hear why Mr Kennedy wants to talk to me privately.' And to talk about themselves, learn more about him, let him know where she came from in terms of family, and what Angus had done to her. Because she would tell him all that, and then he might understand why she'd been so willing to have fun that night they'd inadvertently made a baby. The night when she'd woken up from the apathy Angus had left her with, when her heart had come alive. Still was if the thumping going on was anything to go by. Noah Kennedy did that to her as easily as he'd kissed her. Heat trickled into her cheeks as a wave of longing rolled through her.

'Guess that's my cue to get a wriggle on.' He was watching her too closely, but at least his smile remained. 'I can't believe I've finally caught up with you. It's wonderful.'

Again he'd got to her, softening the tension holding her tight. On again, off again. He was wonderful, and had her dreaming of them being together, close and personal. Nothing like her usual calm disposition.

Show him that and only that side of yourself.

'We could dance around the room.'

Without hesitation, he reached for her, took her hand and one step. 'I'm on if you are.' His smile lightened his face, and lifted her spirits higher. 'You're just as I remember.' He blinked.

Laughter bubbled up her throat as she pulled away. 'That would so not be a good look if anyone walked in. They're already wondering why I'm Anastasia to you.' So was Stacey. It had been a bit awkward when Jason and Liz had commented. She hadn't realised they'd been within hearing distance when she'd talked to Noah earlier, but she should've known. There were no secrets amongst staff on the wards. People were always popping up all over the show, doing their jobs and homing in on background conversations.

Noah nudged the door closed, shutting them into the airless space before tugging her close. 'I once met this amazing Anastasia who loved to dance, among other things, and if I change her name to Stacey that night will fracture.'

She stumbled, ducked away from his hand when he reached to catch her. 'You what?' His memories were that good? This was nuts. They'd had a blast, sure, and she'd been hooked for life, but did *he* really feel it had been so good he didn't want to forget it either?

'How soon can we catch up? I want to talk

with you, see you, hold…' He stuttered to a stop, blinking furiously.

Had he made a mistake, saying that? Her shoulders slumped. Of course he had. But it did seem she rattled him as much as he did her. Something else they had in common, along with understanding each other without explanation. She took the bull by the horns, laid her hand on his arm, breathed deeply, and said, 'Coffee after work tomorrow?'

'Not a mojito?'

Knowing where those led, she shook her head. 'No.' She relaxed enough to grin, though gulping would've been easier. His face wore a teasing expression, but his eyes held a perplexed element to his mirth. It wound her tighter, while heating her blood. This man was a puzzle. She enjoyed puzzles, especially hot, friendly, fun puzzles.

'I'll be finished around six. That work for you?'

'Yes, perfect.' Hopefully her parents would understand and babysit. Today she needed to get home.

To hold my girl and reassure myself I'm about to do the right thing.

'Done. Where's home these days?'

'Same place.' Had she told him last time? 'Harlow.'

The door swung wide and Jason strolled in. 'All right if I grab some lunch?' he asked Stacey.

'Go ahead. We've finished in here.' Ignoring the way Noah lifted one eyebrow in her direction, she headed out. 'Phone me here where to meet you,' she said quietly.

'No problem.' His devastating smile set sparks flicking right down to her toes and all places in between.

By three o'clock and shift handover she couldn't wait to get out of the place, away from constantly looking over her shoulder to see if Noah might've popped onto the ward, even though it was impossible since he was in Theatre all afternoon.

She couldn't believe her luck when there were seats available on the train home. She wouldn't have to swing from the ceiling handles while thinking about the day she'd just had. Sinking down on the seat, she tipped her head back and closed her eyes. Noah was back in her life, this time for a lot longer than one night.

Memories slammed into Stacey. His laugh was her favourite. It made her toes curl and her heart soften when she'd believed that would be impossible. There were the hot, sexy images as they'd danced. Even hotter and sexier ones in that hotel room. Hardly solid proof that he was a good man, the sort of man to be a wonderful father. While gut instinct said he would be, how reliable was that? She could be deluding herself because she was attracted to him. So much relied on her getting this right. So, so much.

Holly's giggling face leapt into her mind, shoving Noah aside. Her little girl, the love of her life.

I promise with all my heart to love and care for you, to do whatever it takes to make you happy and safe, to be the best mother I possibly can be.

The first words she'd spoken to Holly when the midwife had placed her in her arms after the birth. Now she had to tell Noah about his daughter. Yes, she did. All part of the promise to Holly. The sooner the better; get it over and done with. If he really was the man her tingling nerves said he was, then all would be fine. If she found he wasn't, then what? It was highly unlikely and, regardless, he was still Holly's father.

For three years she'd continued checking with friends at other hospitals, and especially those at London General, if they'd heard of him, and come up with *nada*. Every time it'd saddened her, made her think she might never again know the man who'd brought her alive the way he'd done that night. And that Holly would never know her dad.

Now he'd turned up she wasn't quite as prepared as she'd expected to be. Holly should be her main, and only, consideration. She had to be certain her girl would be safe and loved by her father. She would tell him tomorrow night.

Leaping off the train at her stop, she all but ran home, and burst in through the front door. 'Holly! Mummy's home.' Dumping her bag on the floor, she raced through the house, barely able to breathe for the need to hold her girl blocking her throat.

'We're in my office,' her father called.

'Holly, love, where are you?' She shot through the door and scooped her baby into her arms and held her close, brushing kisses over her head. 'Oh, my girl, Mummy loves you so much.'

Holly wriggled and pushed at her mother.

'Sorry, am I holding you too tight?' Stacey loosened her grip but didn't put her down.

At his desk, her father was watching them with a question in his eyes.

She looked away, returned to gazing at her precious girl, who was wriggling harder.

'You want to get down?'

Holly nodded. 'Please, Mummy.'

'Okay.' It was hard letting her go, as though this was a warning of how it might be in the future. Weekends with Daddy, weekdays and nights with Mummy. No way. She couldn't give up any time with her daughter. Her eyes watered as she set Holly on her feet and didn't let go of her arm for a moment too long.

Holly bounced away, leaving her mum's heart cracking.

Her dad stood up and came across the room. 'You've found him?'

'Noah, Dad. His name's Noah.' Her father knew her too well. As long as he didn't see her excitement and bewilderment and start asking unanswerable questions.

'That's a yes, then. I'm glad you're sticking up for him like that. It's a good sign. Where did you bump into him?'

'He's now working at London Riverside. On the surgical ward. He never worked at London General, only went to their ball for his friend's sake.' Her body was shaking, releasing some of the tension that had been growing all day. 'He started while I was on holiday. Who'd have thought after all the trouble I've gone to trying to track him down?'

'You've talked?'

Her head dipped in acknowledgement. 'About patients, about us knowing each other briefly. He calls me Anastasia.' Her voice rose. 'No one calls me that.' But it'd been the only name he knew for her. 'I like it,' she admitted. Then she looked to her father, as she had often in her life, because he'd been her rock whenever things turned to custard. 'Dad, what am I going to do?'

Reaching for her, he wrapped her in a familiar hug. 'You already know the answer to that. You'd have told him years ago if you'd been able to. It's not as if you didn't want to contact him.'

Stepping out of her dad's arms, she sat on the edge of his desk. 'I haven't found out where he's been yet, but when I do I'll brain him for not telling me his full name and phone number at the time.' Finally she began relaxing. 'It's going to be all right.' It had to be. Her gaze swooped over Holly, and her heart clenched with love. 'It will be.' Just who she was reassuring she wasn't sure, but she had to believe it or everything would become a nightmare.

Noah let himself into his house and dropped the keys on the oak side table before heading to the sitting room and a large glass of whisky. What a day. Standing at the French doors leading out onto a patio, he stared blindly at the garden beyond. Anastasia had fallen back into his life. Just as easily as leaves being blown off the trees outside.

Sipping his drink, he tried to empty his head of images of Anastasia. Or Stacey Wainwright. Either version of her name was as pretty as she was beautiful. To him she was Anastasia, and always would be, which suggested he wanted a lot more contact with her now they'd met again. Contact, or something stronger? Deeper?

Could he be overreacting to this stunning woman who came with memories he hadn't managed to delete? Memories that kept him awake some nights, tightening his belly, heating his skin. They'd never faded, not a bit. They'd given him a better reason to return to London than bailing Robert out of the financial debacle he'd got into, even if he hadn't known if he'd find her. She might've even been the reason behind his feeling of missing something important if he continued to stay away.

Yet now Anastasia had resurfaced he was afraid. She might be attractive and funny and delightful, but that wasn't enough incentive to risk his heart. Just because he felt excited at seeing her again, it didn't make her the woman for him. What with moving back into his London house, organising and attending meetings to resolve Robert's financial crisis, as well as taking on the positions as head general surgeon at London Riverside and the private practice, it made sense that his brain was miles behind with what had happened today.

Strange how the years in New Zealand hadn't dampened his need to follow up on that special night he and Anastasia had shared. Her dance moves still turned him on while lying sleepless in the night. His memory drew up more pictures of the woman who'd been so generous with herself and taken all he'd offered with pleasure. Her slim neck had been pale during a London winter with no sun. That thick, dark blonde hair spread across the pillows had tantalised with its silky smoothness. She was a stunner. Then and now. And always smiling. That hadn't changed much either, unless she was with a patient who needed consoling as he'd observed with Jonathon Black.

Why hadn't he taken her phone number? Right now he wanted to hear her voice with its suppressed laughter or full-on happiness. Like the citrus scent, her voice had followed him to the other end of the world to pop into his mind at unexpected moments and fill him with that longing for love he'd known most of his life.

Love. Something he'd had little experience of since his parents had died. At first he'd believed his uncle and aunt would automatically love him, and when they hadn't he'd felt he was somehow lacking. He'd tried harder to please them, only to be sent away to boarding school, where he slaved his guts out to get top grades so they'd come to love him.

When he'd met Christine he'd felt a glimmer of hope, and when they'd married the glimmer had become a beacon. It had never bothered him that she didn't come from money. He'd wanted to share everything he had, especially his heart. But she didn't love him, not in the way he'd anticipated. It was his bank account that had drawn her to him, and she'd made a fool of him with her promises of love. He'd rushed into marriage, wanting to be with someone he believed loved him back, to be a part of their life, to share raising a family in a loving environment such as he'd known for the first ten years of his life. Christine was finally out of his life for ever, and he didn't regret that at all. But he was wiser, warier, and not prepared to try again and come up against a cold heart hidden behind sweet lies.

So, Anastasia. Their encounter had only involved moments on the ward, yet it felt as though a lot more of him had got caught up with her. Which he didn't need. Wrong. He did need what she might have to offer, if it was genuine, and how was he to know that? To trust his own judgement when he'd failed abysmally last time?

Need was one thing, and it was debatable whether he did need her, or if this was unsatisfied lust. But what about want? Did he want her? Impossible to know after such a short time together. Forget his body's reaction to her today.

Just because those feelings of tenderness and longing and heat were the same as last time, they didn't make this a ticket to wholehearted love on both sides.

For all he knew, she might be married, or in a relationship.

What about her shock when she'd turned and seen him? He recognised it for exactly what he'd felt at that moment. Total disbelief, and something like excitement. And, yes, the happiness had been in her face too. They got each other, even after three years. So, now what?

The phone rang. Noah stared at the name on the screen with distaste. The man who'd often said that if his father hadn't married his mother then Dad would still be alive.

'Robert.'

'Noah, you didn't come up to here yesterday as promised. I've been trying to get hold of you all day.'

He hadn't agreed to go, let alone promised. 'I was busy at the hospital.' And talking to interior decorators about making his house a home again after the mess his uncle's sons had left it in. So much for the idea it would be better to have the house in use while he'd been in New Zealand. The refurbishing was going to take months and cost a small fortune.

'Your aunt would like to see you.'

Funny how that was the case now that Robert's many millions had dwindled to a few. 'I'm busy this coming weekend so I'll come the following Saturday if that suits.'

'It'll have to, I suppose. We'll expect you at twelve for lunch.' Click. Gone. Classic Robert, who he no longer called uncle. That was a term for someone he cared about and who cared about him for more than a massive top-up of his bank accounts.

Maybe he should run away with Anastasia and have some fun, like his mother apparently had with his dad. Except running away hadn't been the case. That was Robert's perspective because he lived a 'proper' life amongst snobbish, wealthy folk. His dad hadn't given up his medical career or his home; he'd merely shared everything he'd had with the woman he'd adored. Noah sighed and sipped his whisky. It wouldn't hurt to apply the brakes and take things one day at a time. But it would be hard with his body craving Anastasia. Damn it, for all he knew, she might be hungry for money and happy to do anything it took to get it, including fool him into believing she meant everything she said.

Getting a little carried away here.

But that was what saving his heart had him doing, despite the caution he should be applying.

Though if Anastasia truly had a happy, loving approach to life and could share that with him, he might be more than prepared to take a gamble.

CHAPTER THREE

Stacey got to the hospital early and headed for the cafeteria. 'Toast and tea, please,' she said to the young guy behind the counter.

'I'll bring it over when it's ready.'

'You're a star.' Tiredness dragged at her feet. Most of the night had been spent tossing and turning and wondering how she was going to broach the subject of Holly with Noah. At five, she'd thrown the blanket aside and gone into her daughter's bedroom and stood staring down at the little body of magic. How she'd managed to produce such a gorgeous child was beyond her.

From the day Holly had been born Stacy had been head over heels in love with her, and nothing had changed. Not because she'd had to give up her newly found independence and single life, not because she had to rely on her mum and dad to look after Holly while she went to work and added money to the household. Not because she was so tired at times that she could barely stand up. All of those things and more were worth it just to have her girl in her life.

Sitting down, she checked her phone in case her mum had tried to get hold of her. Nothing. She could relax. Though with Noah back in the picture it wasn't that straightforward. Her reaction to him yesterday had been over the top. Yet she'd loved the excitement pouring into her. He'd rocked her boat the first time they'd met, and yesterday he'd gone and done the same all over again. She could admit to never feeling like that about Angus but, then, they'd been so familiar with each other it probably hadn't been possible.

'Here you go.' Her toast and mug of tea appeared on the table before her.

'Thanks.' A sense of familiarity struck her, warmth and excitement winding her tight and fizzing in her veins. Her skin prickled. Glancing around, she found Noah Kennedy watching from a table across the room with a thoughtful expression darkening his eyes. A shiver rippled through her. She stared at him; really looked at him. Not as a lover, or as Holly's father, but as a man she barely knew yet yearned for in every way imaginable. There weren't enough answers to all her questions in his steady gaze, yet still she believed in him, and wanted more.

Noah got up, mug in one hand, a plate in the other, and came across. 'Mind if I join you?'

'Of course not.'

Far from it. She'd put difficult subjects on hold for now and spend time enjoying his company. Who knew what she might learn? Or she could just spill the beans and see where that went. In here? With someone she knew likely to pop in at any moment? Maybe not.

'You're in early.'

'There wasn't a lot in my pantry and, anyway, hanging around waiting for the toast to burn is a waste of time.'

'You wouldn't think to turn the knob down a little?'

'Knew I should've asked someone how to fix my problem.'

'Where do you live?'

'Bloomsbury.'

No way. Her stomach dropped hard. He was having her on. But looking at him she knew he wasn't. Gulp. 'Nice.' Very nice, if you were into that sort of lifestyle, and she doubted she'd ever be. She was comfortable with little money and a small, crowded house filled with those she loved.

Watching her intently, he said, 'It has its uses, like being close to everything I enjoy about this city, for one.'

'I suppose you don't need a monthly train pass.' She smiled. What did it matter where he lived? Unless he wanted to use that as leverage to gain more access to Holly than she was prepared to give. Her skin prickled. Holly. Caution rose as reality sank in. She really knew very little about this man. Her palms moistened. Was it enough? It had to be. Holly existed. No changing that.

'Trains are the easiest way to get around. No parking worries.' He was still appraising her.

'Is there a problem about something?' May as well be direct.

'Not at all.' The appraisal continued, then he leaned back in his chair with a wry smile. 'Sorry. I'm still getting used to the fact we've met up again.'

She wasn't about to admit to the same thoughts. 'Have you been in London for the last three years?'

'No, I left for Auckland the morning we woke up in my hotel room. I went for a year and stayed three. I hated leaving.'

'Then why did you?'

'Other responsibilities in England.' He turned to look across the room, effectively shutting down the brief conversation.

She studied that strong jawline, the sharp,

see-everything eyes that were the colour of bur-nished steel; the wide chest.

He turned back. 'Now *you're* staring.'

'I am.' And liking what she saw. Her phone vibrated. Mum. She picked it up and tapped the text icon. 'Sorry, need to get this.'

Morning, sweetheart. You left early. Hope you got some sleep and didn't spend all night wor-rying about Noah. Holly's devouring Rice Crisp-ies, with more on the floor than in her mouth.

Smiling internally at the mess she could en-visage, Stacey sent a smiley face and set her phone down to eat some toast. Sensing Noah was watching her again, she looked up. Sure enough, his gaze was fixed on her. Her grin slipped. 'Yes?'

'Can I have your phone number?'

Reality check. It was great he wanted to get in touch with her. She couldn't wait to spend time with him away from here. Telling him about Holly wasn't the issue. She'd decided tonight was the night for that, but—and it was a big one—she just wasn't ready to lose Noah before she'd really found him, as in knowing him bet-ter and letting the passion she felt for him have its head. She was smitten with him, and that was hard to let go of so soon. He'd woken her up, and she'd never gone back to sleep, always hoping he'd return one day. Now he had, and there was a lot on the line.

'Anastasia?' He tapped her hand, lingering over the last touch. 'You don't want to give me your number?'

Shaking her head, she said, 'Of course I do.' She rattled it off and he put it into his contact list, trying to ignore how his finger felt on her skin—hot and tempting.

'I'm messaging you so you've got mine.'
Ping.

Glad to catch up with you.

Deep breath.

Same.

It was true. No matter what lay ahead. Unable to stop herself, she leant forward and touched his fingers, squeezed them lightly.

Noah glanced at his phone, smiled, and stood up, saying, 'See you tonight.' He strode away, totally relaxed. A surgeon with a busy day ahead. A man who touched her like no other and had her smiling even when she was freaking out about Holly. He'd got under her skin and woken her up to new possibilities of love.

It had happened so fast it made it hard to believe it was real, and for the intervening years she'd tried to make herself believe she'd over-reacted to an off-the-scale night. But from the moment they'd bumped into each other yesterday there was no denying she felt warm and excited about the possibilities. She wanted to be with Noah, to really get to know him, while feeling she already did. Was *this* love?

Liz waved from beside the counter and held up a mug. 'Want another?' she mouthed.

Stacey nodded, before surreptitiously running a finger beneath her eyes to remove unexpected moisture before Liz came across and noticed. Love and Noah in the same sentence tickled her insides and had her heart beating wildly. Caution was needed here. Lots of it.

'I see you were enjoying Noah Kennedy's company.' Liz sat down in the seat he'd vacated.

Enjoying? Absolutely. 'It's always good to get to know our specialists a little, don't you think?' Put it back on Liz and hopefully she'd drop the subject.

'You're not fooling me, Stacey. I saw you go all bug-eyed when he was on the ward yesterday.'

'Must've had something in my eye.' She

grinned. What the heck. 'Only reacting as I've been told all the females have since he started.' At least that showed she hadn't got it wrong when it came to Noah's sexy looks.

'Why does he call you Anastasia?'

She'd prepared for this during the night. 'It's my full name, and when we met once years ago, I was sometimes using it.' Once, and only with Noah, but that was for her to know. 'Stacey's a whole lot easier to spell,' she said with a laugh. 'Or so I've been told.'

Liz chuckled. 'Fair enough. So you've met him before and yet you didn't appear to recognise his name. Interesting.'

'It was a brief encounter. You know how those go. Hi, I'm Anastasia. You're...?'

'Where'd you meet?'

'At a dance. He'd come with a friend and didn't know anyone else. We ended up dancing together most of the night.'

'You didn't hang onto him?'

Time to stop this. 'Nope. I had other things going on at the time.' Now drop it. 'Let's go see what we've got this morning.' She stood up.

'Sit down. There's twenty-five minutes before we're due on the ward.'

Sinking down, Stacey gulped coffee and pretended nothing was out of the ordinary with this conversation until it was time to leave.

* * *

An hour after signing on, a patient was brought up from Theatre who'd been taken out by a car on a crossing.

'Miles Canton, thirty-one years of age, fractured femur and hip, four fractured ribs, pneumothorax to left lung and perforated large colon.' The orthopaedic surgeon, Ian Blackwell, had accompanied his patient to the ward. 'He's a competitive cyclist so his fitness will help recovery.'

Stacey nodded, then her breath got stuck in her throat as Noah came up behind Ian. 'Problem in Theatre?' she gasped, unable to stop the thrill cascading through her.

Noah shook his head. 'We're waiting for Theatre to be cleaned up and readied so figured I'd fill you in on the details I had to do with in Miles's case. I've put a tube into the chest cavity. The lung is starting to move. The colon injury was straightforward but nil by mouth until otherwise advised.'

'Of course.' Stacey nodded. 'Liz, I want you with Mr Canton. One on one for today and we'll assess the situation before handover.' Two different and complex sets of surgery on top of each other would have knocked the man around, despite his physical condition. 'There're only two other patients in room three at the moment so put him there so he can sleep.' Fingers crossed.

'Thanks, Stacey. That'll be best.' Noah gave her an appreciative smile.

A smile that sent her heart rate into overdrive. She had it bad. She was only doing her job and yet felt as though he'd complimented her. 'Right, Liz, you're good to go with Mr Canton?'

'On my way.'

Inadvertently she glanced at Noah and saw him watching her with a hint of laughter in his eyes. What was that about? 'Noah?'

'I'd like to see Gloria while I've got a spare moment.' He hustled her along the ward without another word. Thankfully he had enough nous not to take her elbow, and yet she felt as though he'd been about to. That really would have sent everyone's eyebrows halfway up their foreheads. 'How is she this morning?'

'Her wound is healing well, the pain's dropping, though she understands some of the reason is the continuous dosage of morphine. She's chomping at the bit to go home.'

'I'll change the pain relief medication. From what I heard from Joel yesterday, I'm happy to discharge her.' Noah breezed into the room and all conversation amongst the patients stopped as the women looked at him. 'Morning, Gloria.

I hear you're packed and waiting for my signature.' He strode up to her bed.

Stacey resisted winking at the other women and flicked the curtains around them. It was so tempting to be unprofessional because she totally understood their drooling expressions. But she was head nurse and did not want to risk a black mark against her name.

Gloria smiled and looked to Stacey for support. 'Why hang around here when I've got my family waiting for me at home?'

'Is this family going to look after you? Cook your dinner? Make your bed, and generally run around for you?' Noah asked.

'My husband will.'

'Or else?'

'Exactly. He knows when he's onto a winner.'

'I know the consequences if I don't obey she who should be listened to.' The curtain flicked open briefly as Gloria's husband, dressed in a business suit, joined them. 'Morning, Mr Kennedy. Darling.' He dropped a kiss on Gloria's cheek.

'I'm glad you're here, Darryl,' Noah said. 'I'm sending Gloria home, but we need to discuss future treatment.'

'There's always a reality check.' Darryl pulled a chair up to the side of the bed and took his wife's hand in his.

'All right if I sit on the end of the bed?' Noah asked. 'I don't like towering over people when we're talking.'

'Fine.' Gloria's face had lost some colour. Knowing what lay ahead would be daunting, and she'd probably tried to forget all about it for a while.

Stacey filled a plastic cup with water and handed it to her, received a grateful nod.

'First we have to get the site where I removed your breast completely healed. Only then will we start you on chemo. The treatment is exhausting, and it takes its toll on your body, so best to start in as good a condition as possible.'

'How long are we talking?' Darryl asked.

'Six weeks is optimal.' Noah gave them time to think about this, then continued. 'After you've finished chemo we give you a break before starting radiation which is far less distressing. Though I warn you it'll still make you tired.'

Gloria gripped Darryl's hand. 'I do remember the details from when we first came to see you ten days ago, but this is real. Like it's started and isn't over by a long way.'

Stacey looked away from the anguish in the couple's faces. Cancer was a bitch. No other word for it.

Noah was nodding in agreement. 'Most patients say much the same. You're focusing on one day at a time, one treatment at a time. You've had your mastectomy and your body's responding well. Soon we'll move on to the next phase.'

We. He was with them all the way. As they said their goodbyes and headed out of the room, Stacey's heart expanded for this caring man. He really was special. In more ways than one. Could he be a great dad? She believed so. Could he be a great partner? Someone she could trust with her heart? What? She gasped. She'd been thinking how she wanted more from him than just the role of Holly's father. But it was early days. She wasn't falling in love with him. But she'd had strong feelings for him right from that night they'd made love.

'Stacey? You all right?' Noah asked, looking at her as though there was no one else.

Gulp.

'Yes, just…'

Think of something. Quick.

She coughed against her arm. 'I've got a tickle in my throat.'

And I'm lying on a beach in Hawaii, Noah thought.

Something had disturbed Anastasia's usually calm attitude. What'd they been talking about? Gloria's upcoming treatment. Nothing there that he could see to upset Anastasia. 'Are you sure you're okay?' he asked as they walked towards the hub of the ward.

'Like I said, a tickle in my throat.' She was looking anywhere but at him.

Noah breathed deeply. It seemed Stacey could be hiding something but now was not the time to try and find out what. Of course it might not concern him but that gut instinct that came into play around her was knocking hard again, this time negatively. As though he couldn't quite accept Anastasia was nothing like Christine. Or was he trying to find Christine inside her so he could protect himself from getting too involved? Glancing at his watch, he said far more calmly than his heart beat suggested possible, 'I'll drop in on Jonathon while I'm here.'

'Sure.'

They went into Jonathon's room and greeted the patient. 'Morning, Jonathon. I see you're improving fast now we've got that appendix out of the way.'

'I feel better. Has the infection gone?'

'It takes a bit longer than that. The antibiotics are doing their job and I'll be able to lower the dosage within twenty-four hours if this progress keeps up.' He continued asking and answering questions, noting Anastasia was busy avoiding him while being right across the bed and jotting down things he said that were important to their patient's file.

But when they left Jonathon, she murmured, 'Thanks for calling me Stacey on the ward. Most of the time anyway.'

Could that be what was bothering her? That much? All using her full name said to anyone was that they'd known each other before he'd started here. It wasn't enough for her to gasp and lose colour in her cheeks. No, definitely something else was going on, and it involved him, he'd swear, because they were always in sync. Which didn't make sense considering how little they'd had to do with each other. He was probably being paranoid. 'Still on for catching up after work today?'

'Yes, absolutely,' she said quietly. Where had cheerful Anastasia gone?

'I could try to get away sooner since you finish at three. Or you could do what all women I know do when they've got time to kill. Go shopping.' He was beginning to enjoy winding her up.

'Guess you don't know me, then.'

'I'm trying to but you're putting up road blocks.' How much did he want to push this? Hadn't he decided he had a heart to protect? Yes, and he'd also recognised the need he felt when around her had to be looked into further.

Anastasia stopped. Worry darkened her eyes, whitened her lips. 'Noah.' She looked around, then back at him. 'There's a lot you don't know about me.'

'Are you married?' Why hadn't he asked before? Because if she was, he was out of here, no matter what he felt. There wasn't a ring on her finger, but some staff left them at home during working hours.

'No,' she snapped, flicking a look his way he couldn't interpret.

Not married, but maybe not single either? He took another glance, and saw her eyes were narrower and she was entirely focused on the wall behind him.

'What keeps you busy apart from work?' Now he'd started, he wanted to ask more.

'Family.'

She'd shut down. Why? It had been three years since they'd had that time together, and anything could've happened. Where was the harm in asking? He had to look out for himself. She wouldn't have been hanging around all that time on the off chance they'd meet up again. Especially since amazing sex and great dancing were hardly recommendations for a long-term relationship, though he could think of a lot worse. Of course she'd have found a man, but mightn't have reached the stage they were calling it a relationship. It wasn't as though she was unattractive or undesirable, or unfriendly.

There was a strange sensation in the bottom of his gut; like sadness, or was it disappointment? Couldn't be. Now he'd caught up with Anastasia excitement tingled continuously throughout him, like he had something to look forward to. Something warm and caring, not cold and filled with greed.

Okay, admit it. He did want to spend time with Anastasia. Hope for something more with her kept rattling around inside. Not just another one-night stand. He wanted her in his arms, touching her, kissing her. Danger warnings flashed in his head. He could be falling for her, and how would he ever know if he got it right this time? What if she did turn out to be another Christine? Out to get a man who had money to support her and give her a life of luxury, and by chance he fitted the bill? 'You don't live alone?'

After a deep breath, she continued more calmly. 'At the moment I'm living with my parents and brother. Dad had a truck accident and lost a foot a few years back. Since then he's qualified as an accountant and is slowly building up a clientele, but there's not a lot of income coming in. My brother's at university, and Mum works as a receptionist at the local medical centre. I'm supporting them as much as I can.'

Kind and generous as well as fun and exciting. And not well off financially. Yet the tightness in his shoulders backed down after her straight answer. It was hard to hear any falsehood in her voice. 'So no shopping.' Strange how he could smile quite easily now. There was no man in her life. He leaned closer, his gaze fixed on her mouth. Then he jerked upright. What was wrong with him? This was a ward. Stepping back, he hauled in air.

'I get in my fair share, believe me.' She was laughing again, apparently unaware of his reaction to her. Also, surprising how quickly she could restore her good mood. 'There are some great charity shops in our district.'

'You're a recycling fan.'

'Who isn't?'

'When it comes to clothes, you're looking at the ultimate waster of clothes.' Then he went back to her family. 'Your father's accident must've been a hell of a shock for you all.'

'It was, but he's tough, and is truly happy doing what he is. He and my brother attend the same university, and there's always something they're competing over.'

'Your brother's doing a BScs too?'

'Heck no. That would be too much to handle. Toby's doing science.' Pride filled her voice, and her face.

'You love them.'

'Of course I do. And Mum. She's the back-bone of our family, keeps us all on track.'

So simple. Naturally she loved them. No doubts. As he hadn't had any with his parents. His phone vibrated. 'You're very lucky.'

'I reckon. I'd better get back to work.'

'I'll see you later.' With that she headed away.

So they would have time to sit down together and catch up. On what? They only had dancing and sex between them. Yes, but he wanted a whole lot more. He knew that now. He wasn't going to walk away—yet. He had to decide how far to take this, and if he wanted to try again to find happiness. In a very short time, Anastasia had done this to him. Tipped his world on its head.

The phone stopped vibrating. Damn. He'd been distracted. Not good. Unprofessional. Tapping 'return', he waited to find out who needed him.

'Noah, it's Angela. Theatre's ready.'

'On my way.' Time to focus completely and utterly on what he was here for.

As he waited impatiently for the lift, he watched Anastasia talking to Jason. The more he learned about Anastasia, the more his interest grew to find out even more. He was attracted to her. And not only physically. Her smiles blinded him. Her laughter lifted his spirits. Her gentleness and care with patients touched him. She was not a Christine, nowhere near close. She was a giver, not a taker. Yet he couldn't just let go of his hang-ups and dive into a relationship. The past held him back.

What if he never found the kind of all-encompassing love he hoped for? He couldn't settle for second best. That much he did know. Everything else was up in the air. Except that Anastasia turned him on in a flash. She also brought a lightness to his heart he hadn't known before. She seemed to understand him without knowing him. She was special. She looked out for her family, shared their pain and happiness.

But was she worth the risk? Would she hurt him? Everyone in a relationship got hurt at some time or other. It went with living together. But deep, long-term hurt was his biggest fear. He'd survived it when his parents had died, though how, he had no idea, except pure grit, which for a ten-year-old seemed abnormal. It probably came from having no one to stick up for him.

Robert certainly hadn't wanted to hear him cry or talk about how he missed Mum and Dad. His aunt had told him it was natural to feel those things but good people never talked about them. And then there was Christine. He had tried to talk to her about his past and how he'd felt. She hadn't said anything like his uncle and aunt. No, she hadn't said a word at all. Had just asked if he'd finished and picked up her book to continue reading. The Ice Queen.

He should've seen the warning signs then, but he'd been desperate to love and be loved. Before they were married she'd always managed to avoid that conversation, and he'd let her, not wanting to sound like a man who couldn't cope with life. Afterwards he'd wanted to tell her so there were no secrets between them. What a success that had been, but at least he'd finally admitted where he stood with her and had started divorce proceedings not long after. Better alone than ignored.

Anastasia tensed suddenly, as though sensing him watching her. Again on the same page.

He stepped into the lift now open before him and went down to work. That was the cure for most things that ailed him. Work meant getting involved with other people's problems, medical issues. Some were straightforward and had a good ending, some were not. Those were hard to deal with, and often went home with him, waking him in the middle of the night, when he'd think if only he could do more to save these people.

He did all he could, and more, but it would never be enough. Early in his training days he'd learnt to hold himself aloof from others' misery, not to get involved beyond the facts, but he didn't always follow his own rules. Partly because it was impossible, partly because it made him feel he was turning into Robert if he did.

Being around Anastasia might be the best thing to happen. Might turn him around and return him to being more like his mum, as he had been when he'd been little. Hard to imagine being that happy-go-lucky person again. Worth trying for, though. Being happy. Cheerful. Looking forward rather than over his shoulder at the past. Loving someone more than life itself. Even if it meant risking his heart.

Something to think about over the coming weeks. First, he'd meet Anastasia after work.

He laughed out loud as he stood in the lift full of staff. 'Great day, isn't it?' he asked in general, and had to bite his tongue at the ensuing silence.

So he was going mad. Bring it on. It felt far better than the serious life he knew all too well.

CHAPTER FOUR

'I'M AT CONNOR'S CAFÉ.'

Stacey grinned as she did an about-face and strode back the way she'd come to the café she'd passed only minutes earlier. She couldn't wait to see him. So much for common sense. But for sure, she was not losing control with Noah this time. There was too much at stake. Though she couldn't fault her actions last time. She'd had a fantastic night, which had resulted in Holly arriving into her life. Excitement filled her at the thought of being with Noah away from work, however briefly.

'You're looking lovely,' said the man dominating most of her thoughts when she walked up to him at a table tucked into the back of the noisy café where people were eating early dinners. Bending close, he kissed her on both cheeks. 'How are you?'

Worried, nervous, excited. Mostly wound tight with longing. She smiled. 'Happy.' Unless—until—everything came tumbling down around her red-tipped feet. Leaning in close, to feel that lithe body against hers. The need to get even closer overtook everything else. Rising on her toes, she locked eyes with Noah and touched her lips to his. Just like three years ago, her inhibitions were blinded around Noah.

Noah kissed her back, this time longer and deeper, sending her world spinning. Finally he pulled away, leaving her hungry for more of him. 'Your happy disposition is contagious.' His smile was wry. He took her hand and held out a chair with the other. 'Coffee's coming. I also ordered a platter of cheeses and crackers to fill the gap.'

'Thanks. I'm a bit peckish.'

'Me too, and dinner's a way off as I've got a patient to check up on later. He haemorrhaged excessively during surgery.'

Fair enough. She didn't have long to talk to him then. 'Never good. What were you operating on?'

Noah shook his head. 'We're not at work now.'

Nice one. More excitement touched her.

Quieten down, girl.

'Fair enough.'

So what would they talk about? Holly. That was why she'd come. That, and to be with Noah.

'Do you ever think about that night?' Surprise flitted through his expression, as though he couldn't believe he'd asked.

Well, Noah, neither can I.

It was up front and had her wondering where this was going. Another one-night stand? Did she even want that? The moment she'd seen him on the ward she'd felt all those same exciting sensations she'd felt back then, and something more. A connection that really couldn't be explained other than it felt right.

The coffees and nibbles arrived.

When the waitress had gone Stacey told Noah truthfully, 'Yes, I have. Often.'

The surprise lightened. 'Me, too,' he admitted. Then, 'As you were leaving, you said thank you for helping you get on with your life. What was that about?'

Looking into those grey eyes, she found genuine interest, and it gave her a sense of having found a man she could tell her all to. Starting with the truth about her past. 'A year before that dance I was jilted four days out from my wedding.' She stared at Noah.

Don't you dare feel sorry for me, because I no longer do.

'We'd known each other pretty much all our lives, had been best friends and then fell in love and got engaged. When he ended it I was heartbroken, and couldn't seem to get on with my life. One of my friends suggested joining them at the dance and I reluctantly agreed. When I left home that night my father said to go out and enjoy myself, let my hair down—' She stopped when Noah's mouth twitched. 'Guess I did that.'

The twitch became a full-blown grin. 'You did. It was beautiful spread across the pillow.'

She gasped. 'Sure you should be saying things like that? We've only just got reacquainted.'

'It's been two days, far longer than last time.'

'Are you flirting with me?' That was a turn-around from last time.

'Should I be?'

Yes, please.

'Let's wait and see. I had a wonderful night with you, but it was three years ago and who knows if we're even on the same page with our lives any more.'

And there's something huge to tell you.

'At least you're being honest.' That couldn't be relief taking over his expression. He'd started this. 'Something else we have in common,' he added.

She didn't have to ask what else he was referring to. It was there in their easy way together. Funny, but she was completely relaxed, even knowing what lay ahead in the next few days. Stacey looked around the packed room, and then back to Noah. Lifting her flat white, she saluted him. 'I'm glad we've finally caught up. I've wondered where you were, even who you were. You were like a mystery. No one knew you when I asked around. I started thinking I'd made it all up.'

'You tried to find me?'

'I asked everyone from the General Hospital CEO to the janitors. Or close enough. You were a mystery, yet I hadn't imagined that night. Not a minute of it.'

'It was real.' He nodded. 'I asked my friend if he knew you, and I got the same result.'

'It seemed wrong to have such a good time and not follow up, though that might've spoiled the whole thing.' She grinned. 'I was a little tiddly by the time we left the dance.'

He held his thumb and forefinger out, almost touching. 'A little. But you seemed to know exactly what you wanted.'

'No regrets.' Not one. Right, they'd got that out of the way. 'Tell me about your time in New Zealand.'

He filled her in on where he'd lived and worked, and how well he'd got on with his cousin. 'Have you ever been there?'

'I've never left Britain.' Not enough money in the coffers for travelling overseas. 'I've been to Scotland to see where my grandparents came from. Loved all those mountains and lochs.'

'You're a stay-at-home girl? Or travelling not your thing?'

'Angus wasn't into holidays, preferred working on projects, and I guess it rubbed off. No point getting wound up about it when he'd never change his mind.' Though now she questioned her willingness to sacrifice her own dreams for his.

Noah was watching her closely again. 'I've been married.'

Her stomach lurched. 'You have?'

His nod was abrupt. 'Divorced two years before I met you.'

'What happened?'

His mouth flattened, and for a moment she thought she'd gone too far. But he wouldn't have raised the subject if he wasn't going to tell her more. Then he shrugged. 'Christine wasn't who I thought she was. Looking back, I don't think she ever loved me. She wanted the comfortable lifestyle I could provide and in return she offered to have two children in quick succession so we could move on with living the perfect, wealthy life.' Bitterness mingled with anger in his voice, and when Stacey looked into his eyes she saw the same emotions there. 'Like I wanted to have children in those circumstances, without any say in the matter.'

Did he mean he didn't want children, full stop? Or not with his ex? 'I'm sorry. That must've been hard on you.'

'It's fine. I'm over her. Just thought I needed to put it out there.'

Right. He was over his ex? He might not love her any more, but he hadn't got over what she'd done to him. He was where she'd been the night they'd met. Her hopes for tonight and sharing her news dropped. This wasn't looking good for her and Holly. He might not believe her when she said Holly was his. 'Thank you for telling me.'

What else could she say? *I'm here and I wouldn't do that to you. Give me a chance to prove it.*

Noah glanced at his watch. 'I'll have to go shortly.'

Already? 'No problem.' Glancing at the wall clock, she saw they'd spent nearly an hour here. The time had flown by, leaving her hyper and happy, and a little worried. Learning more about Noah was always going to come with pitfalls. Being with him hadn't. The way heat was tripping over her skin had her wishing they could find another hotel room for a few hours. She so wasn't ready to leave Noah, but she was a big girl. She'd get over her disappointment. She hadn't said what she'd come to say either.

'Can we do this again?' How would he take the news of Holly? Until he'd said that about his ex-wife planning on having children in quick succession and hadn't sounded too enthusiastic, she believed he'd accept being a father without too many problems. Now she wondered if she'd got that wrong, and what else wasn't as she thought.

'Absolutely.'

So he was still keen to see her. She exhaled slowly. That had to be good. 'Great.'

'I'll walk you to the station.' Noah stood up.

Brilliant. A few more minutes with him. Despite the children problem, she bounced beside him, like a kid who'd had too much sugar. 'Thanks.' Bundled up in thick jackets, they braved the cold air after the heat of the bar. 'I can't wait for winter to be over.'

'It's been a shock after leaving summer behind down under.' Noah strode out beside her.

Upping her pace to keep up, she shoved her hands deep in her pockets, for warmth and to stop herself from grabbing his hand and holding him until they reached the station. 'You wouldn't think of going back there?'

'It's tempting, but I own family property here that I would never sell. Other people used my house while I was away and I'm now stuck with a massive redecoration project.'

The Bloomsbury house spoke of other-world wealth. No one lived there on a budget. Noah must come from a very wealthy family. Lucky for him. Though nothing like that came without responsibilities, like not being able to live in a country he really liked. His life was nothing like hers, and never would be. It would be great to have a spare few thousand pounds in the bank, but she wasn't in need of a fortune.

From what she'd seen, money didn't necessarily make a person any happier either. With her, Holly would get a grounding in basics such as working for what she wanted. Unless Noah didn't have the same idea and gave her everything. Another thing to find out more about. These few precious minutes were hers to enjoy for herself. 'How handy are you with a paintbrush?'

'A what?' He grinned.

'That good? Fair enough.'

'I'm a doctor. There are qualified painters and decorators to fix my problems while I concentrate on what I am good at.' She waited. Was he going to reveal feelings about that night he wanted to follow up on?

Then he shook his head. 'Another time.'

Her heart sank. 'Okay.'

He touched her jaw, lifted her head. 'Don't worry, Anastasia. I'm not out to hurt you.' His mouth covered hers briefly. Then he took her hand and continued to the station.

At the entrance they stopped, turned to face each other. Stacey gazed at the man who'd changed her life so much without realising any of it and felt comfortable with him. As a thread of warmth wound through her, she had to admit to another feeling—desire. Nothing had changed in that respect. The softening of her stomach, the tightness at her centre, the thumping in her chest—all the same.

How could she feel like that about a man she'd made love with three years ago and not seen or heard from since? Easily, apparently, if the way he made her feel special was an indicator. Did this mean there was more to her feelings than was logical? But it seemed love wasn't logical, could come out of the blue and bang a person over the head like a thunderclap. Not that she *loved* him. But she certainly felt more for him than she'd have believed possible. He was under her skin now, and looked like he was staying there for a long time, if not for ever.

'Anastasia? There was something else you said to me that night.'

She stared at him, hope flickering behind her ribs, her tongue moistening her lips. Did he mean what she thought? What if she uttered those words and got it completely wrong? What was there to lose? Her pride could take a knock. 'Kiss me, please? Again.'

'It wasn't a question last time, it was a demand.' Noah's mouth touched her lips, gently at first, then more demanding, taking over, holding her close, his tongue pushing into her mouth. Kissing her, embracing her.

Weak-kneed, she leaned against him for strength, all the while kissing back with a fervour that brought need cascading throughout her starved body. This was what she'd remembered, and longed for, over and over during the years when only memories had been real. This was why she'd moved on from her past and started looking forward. It was also why she'd never given up trying to find him—for her and for Holly.

But at the moment she relished being with him for herself. She kissed him again and again. This had given her Holly. Their daughter. It could give her a whole lot more if Noah was as invested in her as she was becoming in him.

Stacey paused, and immediately Noah raised his head.

'Anastasia?' He was smiling, his eyes light and sparkling. 'We seem to connect the moment we're alone together, don't we?'

'Alone as in surrounded by others dancing, or people dashing to catch a train? We sure do,' she said with a grin. Leaning back, she stared up at him, and gathered her courage. 'Can I see you at the weekend?' The smile was diminishing, taking her heart with it. She rushed on.

'If it doesn't suit, that's all right.' She wanted to tell him now, but he was heading back to work, and to go with him so they could talk after he'd dealt with his patient didn't sit comfortably. Besides, Toby was looking after Holly while her parents were out, and he wanted to go to see a mate when she got home. Another day would have to do, which wasn't easy now that she'd made up her mind to get it over with.

Noah seemed to be considering his options, making her feel uncomfortable for asking in the first place.

'I know you're busy.'

He reached for her and dropped a kiss on her cheek. 'Stop it. You should come to my house and we'll have lunch.'

'Put like that, how can I refuse?' She smiled.

He answered, 'By saying no.'

'Are you already regretting inviting me? Because if you are, then please say so. But I do want to talk.'

Thump, thump.

She rubbed her chest. 'Spend some more time with you, catching up.'

Noah's eyes followed her movements. 'I am not regretting it. Not at all.'

She gripped his forearm, wished his jacket wasn't so thick she couldn't feel his warmth through it. 'I had a wonderful time with you three years ago, and I wonder what might've happened if we'd stayed in touch.'

'Have you always been so upfront?'

'I'm getting better at it.' Her smile felt strained. Putting in more effort, she looked directly at Noah. 'I'm a late learner about relationships, spending most of my years with one man. There were many signs I didn't see so didn't know to ask about. Learning the truth in such a blunt manner was hard, though probably for the best. I do not want to have that happen again, at least not unless I can say I did everything in my power to prevent it.' She was talking too much maybe, but this was who she'd become and, like she'd said, who she would always be from now on.

'I'm not presuming because we've had a coffee together that we're in a relationship. Not at all. I'd just like to spend some more time with you, and if it isn't what you want then I expect you to tell me.' Where had all that come from? It had nothing to do with Holly, and all to do with herself. Could be she wasn't the devoted mum she prided herself on being. No, not true. But she was entitled to look out for herself in all this as well as for Holly. Anyway, how could she deny the need growing inside her to get closer to Noah? Even while trying to keep on the straight and narrow until everything was sorted between them, she wanted him. Badly.

Noah was looking a little stunned. Then he chuckled. 'Let's have breakfast together in the morning before we start work. Meet at Connor's again. It's between the hospital and the private practice I'm at. Unless you're free in about forty-five minutes? When I've seen my patient?'

Temptation roared through her. There'd be nothing more wonderful than to spend time together, alone, kissing, hugging. Talking about Holly. On her toes, Stacey leaned in and kissed Noah. 'I'll see you tomorrow,' and she tried to step away.

'Not so fast.' His arms wrapped around her, held her hard against his strong frame, and his mouth devoured hers. His tongue tasted her, turning her knees to mush so that she'd have dropped to the pavement if Noah hadn't been holding her so tight. Breathing was impossible. Not that she cared. If she had to die right now, then this was the only way to go. Why had she turned down his offer to go with him?

* * *

Noah watched Anastasia head down the escalator to the trains below ground, his finger touching where her last kiss had landed. 'I'm in trouble.' No matter how sensible he was, how he laid out the facts of his heart not wanting to be broken, or his trust trashed, he was falling for Anastasia Wainwright. He felt like a moth drawn to the light, in danger and unable to back away. It was scary. He hadn't learned enough about her yet.

Should he jump in and risk everything? Stop trying to overthink everything? But what if he'd got it all wrong, and she was another gold-digger? Yet when they were kissing his body was alight with need, and he wanted to rush her off to his bed and make love to her all night long. To enjoy her company, share some laughs and forget he could get hurt again.

When she'd asked to see him again there had been no way he could say no. Open, determined and so lovable, all in one. How could he not want her? Why wouldn't he just fall for her and be done with it?

He'd noticed she'd gone quiet for a brief moment when he'd mentioned yesterday where he lived, and then tonight when he'd told her the house needed redecorating there'd been another quiet moment, but he didn't think that meant she was calculating his worth, however little she knew. From what he'd seen and heard about her lifestyle with her family, he understood there wasn't a lot of money to spare, but he couldn't believe she would be someone to grab at him for what he had. Of course, he'd got that wrong once before.

Sighing, he turned in the direction of the hospital. A patient required his attention, and he required some work to silence the doubts and arguments cramming his head.

And in the morning they'd have breakfast together. It couldn't come fast enough and wouldn't be anywhere as much time with Anastasia as he'd like.

'Noah, wait.'

He spun around and caught Anastasia as she bounded up and threw her arms around him. 'I can't stay all night.'

Noah kissed her like his life depended on it. Then he drew back. 'Guess we'd better get a move on then.' The hospital visit wouldn't take long and then they'd grab a cab to his house. His blood was throbbing in his wrists and making his head light. Gripping her hand, he almost dragged her to the hospital and into the lift.

And finally, after making certain his patient was doing as well as expected, Noah took Anastasia out again onto the street to wave down a cab and take her home, kissing all the way.

Inside the front door, he leaned back to nudge it shut, Anastasia in his arms. 'Welcome to my house.'

She didn't stop to look around, just rose up on her toes and wound her arms around his neck. 'Run out of kisses?'

'Not likely.' And he lost himself in her arms, until he had to possess her. Swinging her up into his arms, he strode along the hall and into the sitting room to the sofa. When he laid her down, she remained holding him, keeping him close, her fingers working magic on his shoulders, reminding him of how she made him feel soft and hard, hot and strong whenever her fingers were on his skin. 'Anastasia, slow down.'

'Can't.'

Neither could he, unless she wanted him to, and it seemed she didn't. So he went with the passion rising throughout him, touching her soft, warm skin, caressing, sucking her nipples until she cried out. Somehow they were naked, though he couldn't recall removing any clothing, and he lay back with Anastasia on top of his pulsing body as she rolled a condom over his erection. Her legs were spread wide, her centre beckoning with heat and moisture, and then they joined. Anastasia's back arched under his hands, her head tipped back and that satiny hair skimming his thighs as they came.

Noah sank into a haze of release and satisfaction. This was what he'd been hoping for ever since Anastasia had walked out of his hotel room three years ago. Anastasia was his dream. With her, he lost all sense of everything but her. And it felt right. Good. Beyond good. Unreal.

Careful.

Sure, but not tonight.

His mind slipped back to when they'd met. He'd tried not to stare down at the petite woman beside him as they'd strolled into the hotel foyer to take a break from the loud music. She'd been impossible to ignore, having intrigued him when he'd seen her dancing on the perimeter of the dance floor. He'd never forgotten the way her hips had had his mouth drying faster than a puddle in the desert as she'd swayed in time. The colourful skirt had accentuated her delightfully curved butt, while her tiny waist gave way to breasts that had his hands itching to touch them. She had an urchin look. As for those brown hazel eyes, they'd snagged him every time she'd looked directly at him. And in every dream about her he'd had since.

Now here they were, sprawled across his sofa, exhausted from making love, and he was ready to do it again. His lips touched her forehead. 'Hey, you awake?'

Her mouth spread into a wide smile, lifting at the right corner, while her eyes filled with mischief. 'You're a lot better than that.'

He laughed. 'You say the nicest things.' He leaned in for another kiss. A simple yet intense kiss that rocked him on his firmly placed backside. A kiss that was rapidly heating his blood and banishing the lethargy following their love-making.

Her arms tightened around him, her breasts pressed closer, her thighs also.

On her face he saw a similar need to what was knocking at him, turning him into a pool of desire. He was a goner. 'Anastasia?'

She nodded slowly. 'Noah.' When she growled his name into his mouth he almost came before she did.

Anastasia.

It was over as fast as it started, and this time they sat up, leaning back against the sofa, until their breathing returned to normal. Then her phone pinged, and she stood up, taking his hopes with her as she began tugging on her clothes. As though she knew who'd messaged. 'Sorry, but I need to get home.'

'You can stay the night,' he said, trying not

to sound needy. Or worried there was someone else in her life after all.

She shook her head. 'Not tonight.' The light was gone from her eyes, replaced by what? Disappointment? Regret? Yes, that was it. But why? Or someone else she'd just let down? She'd made love so acceptingly. Taking and giving. Completely involved.

'You are single, are you?' he demanded, suddenly on edge about her hurried departure.

Contrition blinked out at him. 'Yes, Noah, I promise I am. I would never play around on anyone.'

His lungs let out the air they'd been holding. He nodded. 'I believe you.' Without question, which only showed how involved he was getting.

'Thank you. I have to get home to cover for my brother.' Bending down, she kissed his forehead. 'See you tomorrow for coffee?'

'Definitely.' He stood up. 'I'll walk you to the station.'

'That's not necessary.'

'Nevertheless, I'm doing it.' Taking her arm, he led her to the front door, and down to the street. At the station he kissed her gently. 'Until tomorrow.'

Anastasia smiled up at him, all trace of her previous rush to get away gone. 'I'm glad

I've found you.' Then she whirled around and headed down the stairs to her train.

Noah followed her every step until she'd disappeared from sight, his heart pounding as longing for a full and happy life gripped him. 'I can't wait to see you again.' What was astonishing, he really meant it.

Friday morning in the staff cafeteria, Stacey fiddled with her mug of coffee, twisting it back and forth between shaky fingers. Those few snatched hours with Noah on Tuesday night had been wonderful and had proved she hadn't been exaggerating her memories. He made her feel special and happy being with him. If only she could've stayed all night. Leaving had been hard, but essential. Not so much Toby grizzling by text she was late, but the fact she and Noah hadn't talked about Holly, and hadn't been likely to if she'd stayed, had brought on a bout of guilt and had had her heading home where she'd lain awake most of the night, reliving their love making.

'Morning, Anastasia.' The man of her dreams slid onto the chair opposite her. 'How're you today?'

Tired, worried and… 'Happy to see you.'

His eyebrows rose, followed by a soft smile

that did nothing to stop her wanting him. 'You're easily pleased.'

'I am.' That depended on the problem.

His brow knotted. 'Why? Don't you want a lot more in your life?'

Was he talking wealth? Of course he was used to it and probably had no idea how other people got by without bemoaning the world for their lot. So much for that smile turning her into jelly. He'd got serious very quickly. 'Like what, Noah? My family adores me, I have the job I've always wanted. I'm not incarcerated in the house when I'm not working. My parents aren't dragons and I can come and go as I please.' With her finger, she drew a circle on the table. 'What goes around comes around. Sure, one day I'd like a home of my own, and a man to share it with, but right now I have nothing to complain about.'

'What about a new car or a holiday?'

She dug up a smile and went with honesty. There was no other way to deal with his doubts and if he couldn't see the truth hitting him over the head then they weren't as suited as she was starting to think. Maybe she'd been blindsided by wishful thinking. They were poles apart in just about every facet of life, except for dancing, kissing, making love—and a child. 'I'd like those things, but I can live without them.'

'Without regrets.' He nodded.

'Totally.' Was he checking out her reaction to his house last night? She'd been so focused on Noah, she'd hardly taken any notice except it had felt large and spacious.

The girl from behind the counter appeared at their table with Noah's breakfast. 'Here you go.' She smiled coyly.

'Thank you,' he acknowledged the girl with a pleasant smile, nothing like the stomach-twisting ones he gave Stacey. Turning his attention back to her, he said, 'Your own house and man, huh?' Then he smiled and she relaxed a little.

'Naturally. And a family.' The words slipped out before she knew she was going to say them. Testing the waters? Might as well go for broke. 'Do you ever think about having children? I know you said your wife wanted to have two, but you sounded as though you weren't interested.'

The smile slid off his face. 'Isn't this a bit soon to be talking about having children?'

'Says the man who just questioned how comfortable I am in my less than well off life.'

Putting down his knife and fork, Noah reached for her hand. 'I'm sorry. You're right, I did speak out of turn. So, yes, one day I would love to have a family, but not when I'm told to, and how many and what to name them before they're even conceived. Children should be a delight, not a duty.'

Stacey sat back, watching Noah as he returned to eating his bacon and eggs, her own scrambled eggs not looking so enticing any more. Which category did Holly fall into? Delight or duty? Only one way to find out and she wasn't about to tell him when they had to get to work shortly. He'd need time for reality to sink in, and then she'd have to answer a load of questions. Clock-watching wouldn't help. And since she couldn't change that, she ignored the gremlins holding her tight and said, 'What time shall I come into town tomorrow?'

'How about I pick you up at home and we go somewhere out of the city?'

The egg slid off her fork.

You can't come to the house with Holly there. Not until we've talked. Quick, think.

A phone rang quietly. Not hers. Saved.

Noah tugged his from his shirt pocket. 'Guess that's breakfast done.' He held it to his ear. 'Noah Kennedy.'

Despite her nerves, a thrill ran down her spine as she thought back to the day they'd first spoken on the phone. That deep voice had got her wondering if she knew the man on the other end and had made her skin tingle. Then she'd met the man behind the voice and everything had changed. Here was Noah, after all this time, and she had to pinch herself every day to make sure she wasn't dreaming. He was as exciting and hot as she'd remembered. Tuesday night had only enhanced everything she adored about him, and while they had a lot to talk about there was no quietening the need for him that kept her filled with desire and hope.

'An elderly man fell down the stairs at an underground station and needs surgery for a perforated lung. See you tomorrow. I'll wait for you at the station near my house.' He was stuffing the phone back in his pocket as he stood up, his mind obviously on the patient ahead, and not her and their date.

Without uttering a word, she'd got over that hurdle. 'Can't wait,' she said honestly.

Noah came towards her. 'Anastasia, you are special. Not everyone appreciates what they have as much as you do.' With that he was striding away, leaving his half-eaten breakfast and her bewilderment behind.

So he hadn't been totally diverted by that phone call. Did that mean he hadn't realised she was avoiding him going to Harlow to pick her up? If so, she wouldn't get away with it for long, but then she was going to reveal all in the morning anyway. Noah. The man who lifted her spirits just by being himself.

He probably didn't realise she was keen on him, other than to make love to. Or he did and was taking his time revealing his own feelings. What *did* he feel about her? Lust? Or more? She was being impatient. She still wasn't totally certain how deeply she felt for him. All she knew was that she wanted more of him, more with him, more, more, more. His kisses spoke of need and desire, but was there something behind those that spoke of emotions that encompassed her?

CHAPTER FIVE

ON SATURDAY NOAH waited impatiently for Anastasia to arrive, scanning every face coming up the stairs. In his hand was a large black umbrella as outside the entrance rain bucketed down, filling the drains to overflowing. So much for a drive and lunch out in the countryside.

Anastasia had said she'd text him when she got to the station, but hanging around waiting at home had been impossible. Now he paced up and down, dodging other people almost as impatient for the train as he was. Bet they didn't have a gorgeous woman coming to see them, or dance music ready to play and mojito ingredients on the bench, or clean sheets on the bed. Did he have it bad, or what?

He wasn't going to rush her to the bedroom; he was being prepared, that was all. No denying he'd wanted her since the moment she'd turned to look at him in the ward on Monday, and making love the other night hadn't been nearly enough. Even better, Anastasia seemed to reciprocate his feelings. There were many doubts about their future, but he needed to see them through, to make sensible decisions, and to do that he had to get to know her better, and yet the moment he was with her he gave in to the clawing need only Anastasia brought on.

'Hi.' A soft hand slid into his, jerking him back to the present. Then those soft lips he dreamed about brushed his mouth.

Noah groaned and pulled Anastasia into him, returned her kiss with vigour. This was what he'd been waiting for. 'Morning to you, too.'

Under his mouth, she laughed. 'We're crazy.' Then she moved back and looked at him intently, the smile dimming, concern in her eyes. 'I take it we're going to your place now that the weather's changed?'

'Yes, unless you don't want to.' Why wouldn't she? It was more relaxed and intimate than going to a café or bar. 'What's up?'

Anastasia straightened. 'Nothing. I'm pleased we're not going out in this, that's all.'

'Would you prefer to go to a restaurant or bar?'

Her smile returned. 'No, not at all.'

He could relax. Flicking the umbrella open and holding it above them, he took her hand in his free one. 'Let's go.'

Keeping in step with him—like their dancing—she leaned close, stayed close as they splashed through puddles along the footpath. Then she hesitated. 'That man under the shop overhang. He looks…'

'Very unwell, like—'

'He's having a medical—'

'Event. Heart attack?'

They ran, stopped in front of the man slumped against the wall, one hand gripping his upper left arm.

'Sir? I'm Noah Kennedy, a doctor, and Stacey here's a nurse. Are you all right?' The guy was grey and shaking.

'It's my arm. Pain.'

'He's sweating profusely,' Stacey noted. 'I'll call an ambulance.'

'Can you get us a chair from inside as well, please?' Then to the man, 'We need to get you sitting down. What's your name?'

'Len.'

'Any history of heart disease?'

'No. The pain's in my arm, not my chest.'

Heart attacks often presented first as pain in the left arm. 'Any tightness in your chest? Difficulty breathing?'

'It feels strange, and sometimes I can't take a full breath. My jaw's hurting.'

'Here.' Stacey was back with someone from

the shop carrying a chair. 'The ambulance is on its way.'

Noah helped Len onto the chair and knelt beside him. 'Take it easy.' It'd be better to be inside, but he wasn't having the man walking anywhere when his heart was playing up. That it was a heart attack wasn't in doubt, and all they could do was take obs and watch closely until the paramedics arrived, be prepared if Len's heart stopped.

Stacey had her phone on timer and was counting Len's pulse rate. 'One twenty.' Then she was onto the respiration rate. 'Abnormal.'

Noah nodded. 'Thanks.'

Her slight nod told him she was up with the diagnosis. They worked as a team, neither having to ask anything of the other. Could they work together as well in their private lives? So far they were in sync about most things, so why not? Was that what real love was about? Having each other's backs without being asked? Understanding where each was coming from and going with it? Sounded wonderful. If it was true. And so far it seemed to be. A wailing siren reached his ears, and relief took over. 'That was quick.'

Stacey was holding Len's hand, her finger on his pulse again. 'It's your lucky day, Len.'

'You think?' The man gave her a wry smile. 'Thanks for noticing me.'

'Not a problem,' they said in unison.

Noah laughed. How like them.

Within minutes they'd handed over to the paramedics and were on their way to his house.

'I'm so glad we noticed Len's distress. Most people wouldn't have thought he was in difficulty,' Stacey muttered.

'True, but we're trained to be medically observant.' At home, he took Stacey's sodden jacket to hang on the stand. She needed a decent leather one to keep dry and warm. 'You're shivering.'

She stepped up to him, warmth in her eyes at least. Winding her arms around his neck, she stretched up to kiss him. 'Then warm me up.'

'Cheeky.' Noah held her tight. This was becoming normal—the excitement, the being together, the enjoyment of each other. He could go with it, was starting to see they might have a future that didn't hold doubts and fears, that he might find the love he'd been looking for. And it had all started with a dance. 'Come on. We'll have some fun.'

Her eyes lit up. 'We're good at that.'

He couldn't help himself, he just had to kiss her again, and again, and hold her curvy backside in his palms, and kiss a trail down her neck

to that alluring cleavage, and help her shrug out
of her jeans, and pull her jersey over her head.
And help her push his jeans down to his thighs
and then to his knees and ankles so he could
step out of them. Tugging his jersey and shirt
off in one swoop, he scooped her into his arms
and headed upstairs where he laid her on the
bed and lay down with her.

Anastasia rolled onto her side and reached for
him, the desire in her face heating him further
and making his heart swell with need and care
for this wonderful woman. Up on his arms, he
covered her gently, and tasted her from top to
toe and back again. Her frantic gasps and cries
drove him to the edge, and then he was filling
her, taking her, giving to her, and they were one.

Stacey's favourite dance tune cut through the
blur in her head. She was dreaming. She and
Noah were dancing. No, they weren't. She could
feel his naked body lying the length of her lan-
guid leg, hip, arm.

'You going to turn that off?' Noah grunted
beside her.

It was her phone. Not music playing in the
background as they'd made love. Sitting up,
she stared around the room, spied her bag on
the floor. As she dug the phone out the music
stopped. 'No need.' Dropping the phone on top

of her bag, she lay down again, and splayed her hand over Noah's chest, absorbed his heat.

The music started up again. 'Go away, whoever you are.' Reaching for the phone to shut it down, she froze. 'Mum?' Her family knew she was with Noah and that today was the day to tell him about Holly so Mum wouldn't ring unless it was urgent.

'I have to get this.'

Noah sighed. Fair enough. This had spoiled a wonderful moment between them.

Hopefully he'd understand later. 'Mum? What's up?'

'It's Holly. She's had an accident and is on her way to hospital in an ambulance.'

'What? Holly's hurt?' Stacey shrieked. 'No, Mum, please, don't say that.' Her head spun so fast she had to lean back against the headboard. Not her girl. No, anything but that. 'What's happened? Is she going to be all right? Tell me. Who's with her?'

'Dad's with her. She ran into the road after her ball. The kids from next door brought us some eggs and left the gate open.' Her mother hesitated.

Stacey's fear cranked up harder. 'Mum? Please tell me she's all right.'

'A boy on a skateboard knocked her over. The ambulance crew think her arm is broken.' A deep breath and her mother raced on. 'She hit her head when she landed and lost consciousness for a while. There's a cut along her hairline above her forehead. Oh, darling, I'm so sorry this has happened. Those kids know to shut the gate, but I should've checked.'

'It's not your fault. I have to get to Holly. Which hospital? Noah can drive me there now. Did she regain consciousness?' Out for a while. What did that mean? Still out? Stacey scrambled to her feet, leaned against the wall to steady her wobbly legs, and swallowed hard. Her voice was rising uncontrollably. 'Tell me. Has she regained consciousness at any time? Is she in pain?'

'Anastasia? What's happened? You look terrible.' Noah stood before her, reaching for her arm.

'Mum?' she pleaded, grabbing Noah's hand, holding it tightly as she said to him, 'There's been an accident.'

'I think so. It was hard to tell but I saw her eyes open briefly and she was staring at her granddad for a moment.'

Was that consciousness or a reaction to a severe head injury? 'I'm on my way.'

'Anastasia, what's going on?' Noah demanded.

Pulling her hand free of Noah's, she started tugging on her clothes. 'I have to go to the hospital near home. Now. Holly's been in an accident.' Her voice was shrill. Fear clawed through her. Her baby was hurt and she wasn't with her, wasn't holding her, couldn't encourage her to be all right. 'Come on, Noah. Hurry.'

Noah shrugged into his clothes. 'Who's Holly?'

Not now. This wasn't how she was supposed to tell Noah he was a father. 'Mum, we're coming. Where are you?'

'Behind the ambulance. Toby's driving us. He raced out when he saw Holly head down the drive, but he was too late to stop her being hit.'

'He tried.' She shoved the phone in her bag. Toby would be gutted. He adored his niece— watch out anyone who hurt her.

'Anastasia, let's go.'

'Would the train be faster?' she cried as they ran down the stairs. Holly dominated her thoughts. Nothing, no one else mattered.

'Fifty-fifty, and we'd have to get to the hospital from the station.' It seemed like seconds and hours before she was belted inside Noah's four-wheel drive and he was pulling away from the kerb. 'Which hospital?' he asked.

Huddling down in the seat, she told him, and wished the trip to be fast and uneventful. 'Thank you for doing this.'

'Why wouldn't I take you to whoever has

been injured when it's so obvious that person is very special to you? We can do lunch any time.'

Her tongue stuck to the roof of her mouth. Fear sat like a lead ball in her stomach. Sweat broke out on her brow. Clasping her hands tight, she stared at the road unfolding ahead of the car. Tense silence filled the air between them.

'Stacey?'

When he flicked to the shortened version of her name it put her off track. She didn't know the reason behind it, except it seemed he'd done it to get her full attention.

Here we go.

'Holly. My daughter.'

'You have a child?'

'Yes.'

'You've never mentioned her.'

'We haven't spent much time together.'

'I'd have thought a daughter would be the most important topic of discussion no matter where we were. In the café the other morning, on the ride up here, having a coffee and nibbles at the cafe. You mentioned your family. Surely family includes your daughter?' Noah sounded cross and confused, as he had every right to be.

In normal circumstances she'd have bored him silly, talking about Holly. Now she had to tell the truth, but while they were racing for the hospital? It was too much. Yet she needed his strength and support. What if he dropped her off at the hospital and she never saw him again, except at work? He wouldn't do that. He'd want to meet his daughter. No doubt about that.

'I'll ask once more. Is there someone else in your life? Someone important?'

'Only Holly.'

You can do better than that.

'I've been single for years, and not dated much. Being a mum takes most of my time when I'm not working.' Was Holly's accident payback for not being there? She shouldn't have come out today, should've been at home, playing with Holly, then this insane ride mightn't be happening. She should've talked to Noah the moment she'd arrived at his house, not got distracted making love. Holly, her beautiful, trusting little girl.

Your mother's stuffed up, sweetheart.

'Holly, hang in there. Mummy's coming.'

She didn't know she'd said that out loud until Noah placed a hand on her clenched fists. 'Easy. I'm getting you there as fast as I can.'

'I know, but it'll never be fast enough. I have to be with my girl.'

'Do you know what happened?' At least he was sounding friendly, though a bit cautious. And he was here for her, getting her to the hospital fast.

'The kids next door left our gate open. Holly chased her ball out onto the road and a boy on a skateboard collided with her.' Anguish gripped her, pain tightened her heart. 'I should've been there,' she cried, turning her hands, loosening her fingers to grab Noah's. 'What sort of mother am I to go out and leave her at home?'

'She was with your parents, wasn't she? No mother spends twenty-four seven with their child. It's not normal or good for them. You're allowed time out, Stacey.'

Stacey, huh? She wasn't getting her head around why he'd swapped between the versions of her name. 'You're right, but I can't accept it. She's on her way to hospital,' she cried.

Removing his hand, he said, 'Tell me about her.' He was concentrating on the road and the busy traffic ahead and swallowing hard.

Was he starting to wonder if Holly was his? He couldn't be. He didn't know how old she was.

I want to tell him. But not right now. Not when he's driving and I can't look into his eyes to show I am not lying.

Not when she was desperate to be with Holly, and nothing else mattered as much.

'Is she cute, and funny like her mother?' Noah seemed to have accepted she was a parent. Or was he just doing the right thing in trying to distract her from her pain on this *far too slow* journey?

'Holly's gorgeous. Her favourite stories are about fairies, and pink is the only colour she'd wear given half a chance. She doesn't have a dancing bone in her body, but that doesn't stop her trying. And wiping out the coffee table in her attempts.'

'Not entirely like her mother, then.' There was a hint of a smile in Noah's voice.

She still couldn't relax. 'Everything's an adventure, especially digging the veg garden with Granddad. He has a special patch where they plant carrots and radishes and peas that's Holly's garden.'

'Is she the reason you're living with your parents?' He was back to driving with two hands on the steering wheel, his knuckles white.

'Yes. Mostly.'

Holly.

'She's got to be all right.' She needed to explain, to tell Noah everything. Her heart was breaking, and her head aching. She just wanted to get to Holly and hold her—if she was able to. At least she'd hold her hand and be there for however long she was in hospital. She stared at the dark screen on her phone. Why wasn't Dad ringing? Did that mean bad news? Surely Mum had reached the hospital by now? She'd phone no matter what. Wouldn't she? 'Can we go any faster?'

'Not legally, no.' But the car lurched forward as the speed picked up.

Closing her eyes, Stacey leaned back and let Holly fill her mind. Laughing as she played with her favourite doll. Grinning when she ate ice cream in a cone and got more on her face than in her mouth. Crying when she'd had three stories at bedtime and wasn't allowed *one* more. Cuddling into her mum, thumb in her mouth, and watching TV.

'What are her injuries?'

'Suspected broken arm and head injury. She lost consciousness for a while.'

Noah was rummaging around in the side pocket of his door. 'Here.' He handed her a small packet of tissues.

Still being a gentleman after his idea of who she was had been tipped upside down. Couldn't ask for better than that. Not that she'd be asking for anything from him except understanding, and it was too soon for that. There was a lot for him to get his head around once he understood Holly was also his daughter. It wouldn't be easy to take in. He'd have lots of questions, and she'd do her utmost to answer them. Stacey's heart ached for this man she'd placed so much hope in.

'Th-thanks.' He might never understand or forgive. Though she wasn't really guilty of anything. The pregnancy had been an accident. One she had been thrilled about once she'd got over the shock.

Tapping her mother's speed-dial number on her phone, she barely waited for her to answer before demanding, 'Have you heard anything from Dad?'

'Not a word, but he might not be allowed to phone while in the ambulance.'

Highly unlikely, but she'd not say so. All she could do was hope her father's silence was good news, that maybe he was too busy holding Holly to call. 'How far from the hospital are you?'

'Pulling in right now.'

'Give Holly a kiss from me if you see her before I get there.'

'Will do. Travel safely.'

'We are.' She looked sideways at the man rushing her to her daughter. He was a steady, capable driver, concentrating on getting them to hospital quickly and safely. Not bad considering what must be going through his mind. Holly could do worse for a father.

Noah whipped into the first available space in the staff parking lot, put his surgeon's pass on the dash, and leapt out of the car. Stacey wasn't going inside alone. He'd be with her until she met up with her parents. Despite her stunning news about her daughter, he couldn't leave her alone. She was distraught, and needed someone at her side. Even him. Admittedly, he was angry she'd not mentioned she had a child at any moment in their time together. It was as though she'd been hiding Holly from him. But why? Having a daughter didn't mean he'd stop seeing her.

So far he thought she'd always been honest about everything. Unlike Christine who'd lied about loving him, about just about everything. Anastasia might be just as adept. Time for questions later. She was already half out of the car as he strode around to join her. Putting on his best *don't argue* voice, he said, 'I'm coming with you.'

'Thank you.' She reached for his hand and dragged him along at a fast clip.

As easily as that Anastasia had accepted his presence. Because she needed him especially? Or would she be grateful for anyone to accompany her? That didn't add up considering how close she seemed to be to her family. She always talked about them with love in her voice, and that touched a spot inside him that held envy and longing. She had what he craved, and he wanted to share it with her. Yes, with Stacey.

He was willing to give it a try, to put the past behind him, forget how he'd been lied to, and give this wonderful woman every chance possible. He stretched out his steps to keep up with her. They were on a mission. 'We'll go straight to the emergency room.'

'Where else would I be headed?'

Noah realised he was out of his depth here. He wasn't a parent rushing to his injured daughter. Squeezing Stacey's hand, he said nothing more, but he didn't stop thinking about Stacey and the pain she was going through. If only he could take it away—or take it on himself. But all he could do was be there for her, and in a few minutes she'd have her family surrounding her and he'd become redundant.

I don't want that.

The idea of being left out in the cold already made him shiver. Anastasia had got to him far more than he'd been prepared to admit. Today, seeing her agony, had woken him up, despite his misgivings about why she hadn't talked about Holly. Bottom line, he could no longer deny she was becoming important to him.

'Hurry up,' Stacey yelled at the slowly opening sliding doors at the entrance to the emergency room. She pushed through, still dragging him along, and headed to the reception desk. 'I'm Stacey Wainwright. My daughter, Holly, has been brought in by ambulance in the last twenty minutes,' she snapped.

Her hand was trembling in his. He stepped nearer. 'Steady.'

The woman behind the counter was looking at the screen in front of her. 'Holly Wainwright, date of birth?'

Noah listened as Stacey gave Holly's birth date. The door beside them clicked as the lock opened. 'Go through.'

Holly was two? That meant she'd been conceived after their night together. So there had been someone else, despite her denial. Not much dating, she'd said, but it only took once to get pregnant. His feet were leaden as he walked beside her. She'd become a mother since he'd first known her. That was hard to accept. As if he'd been abstaining throughout those years. There hadn't been cause to, but neither had he had many dates.

But— But he was being arrogant. She was entitled to live her life however she wanted, and he certainly couldn't complain. She'd said she was single, so he didn't have to walk away without seeing if they'd be a match. He just had to get over himself.

'Dad,' Stacey shrieked, pulling away from him and racing to the man standing by a cubicle. 'Where's Holly?'

The composed nurse he knew had flown out the window. Which warmed him. This was the Anastasia he'd always wanted to believe in. Nothing like his cold uncle and aunt. He'd at first tried to deny Stacey's loving warmth because that meant letting her in more than she'd already managed to get.

Her father nodded to the bed beyond the curtains, and Stacey disappeared out of sight.

Stepping up to the man, Noah put his hand out. 'I'm Noah Kennedy. Anastasia was with me when her mother phoned about the accident.'

The guy glanced at his daughter and then looked hard at him, a question in his gaze. The question slipped away, replaced with welcome. Finally he shook Noah's hand. 'Yes, we knew who she'd gone to see. Nice to meet you, Noah. I'm Ian Wainwright, and this…' he turned slightly '…is my wife, Stacey's mum, Judy. And our son, Toby.'

Judy was staring at him, caution couldn't be more direct on her face. Why were these two so wary about a man their daughter had been out with that morning? Were they overly protective? It wasn't his place to comment, and he could be totally off track about this family. Anastasia never spoke of them without love. Did she know how lucky she was? Yes, she probably did. He held his hand out to Judy. 'Pleased to meet you, Mrs Wainwright.'

The woman before him blinked, also looked at her daughter before coming back to him and taking his hand in hers briefly. 'Hello, Noah. Thank you for getting Stacey here so quickly.'

Noah managed a small laugh. 'Anyone would have done the same.' Then he turned to look at Stacey, and his heart stuttered.

She was sprawled on the very edge of the bed, her hand holding her daughter's and wearing a strained smile. 'Darling, it's Mummy. I'm here, baby.' She was blinking rapidly, trying to keep the tears at bay.

The girl was tiny in the large bed, her face abnormally pale with streaks of dried blood from her forehead staining her cheeks, and her eyes were closed, long, dark lashes black on that wan skin. She looked so fragile Noah felt his heart crack. For Stacey, and Holly.

Someone cleared his throat. 'Excuse me, I'm Dr Robinson. Harry Robinson. I've arranged for a CT scan of Holly's head,' he said directly to Anastasia. 'The paramedic said she was in and out of consciousness on the way here, and so far she's not responding to anything. I'll explain all the scenarios to you. She's also broken her arm, though an X-ray will confirm that.'

Judy said, 'Stacey's a nurse. She'll know what's going on.'

Stacey's head whipped up. 'Right now I'm a mother, not a nurse.' She nodded to Harry Robinson. 'Talk to Noah. He's a doctor. He can tell me what I need to know.' And she went back to gazing at her daughter, imploring silently for her to wake up.

Noah wanted to hug them both, hold them until this nightmare was over and they could all go home. Instead, he straightened his shoulders and faced the other doctor. 'Harry, tell me what you know.'

They stepped aside and instantly Stacey's parents moved up to the bed, where Judy began smoothing Stacey's hair with long strokes that spoke of love.

Noah watched them as he listened to Harry.

'Certainly concussion. I'm worried there might be swelling on the brain. The non-response has gone on too long.'

'Given she's only two, that might work in her favour, keep her still while everything settles down.' But the idea of brain trauma made him ill. This was Anastasia's daughter, she didn't need anything so awful happening to her girl. No parent did. But today, with the woman he was beginning to care too much for, it went beyond his normal horrified reaction for any par-

ent whose child was suffering. He didn't want
Holly injured. He didn't want Anastasia suffering for her daughter. They didn't deserve this.

Somehow he managed to listen to all the details Harry gave him. Stacey was right. It was
different when the patient was close to you, and
though Holly wasn't his daughter and he'd never
met her, he felt a part of this family at the moment.

'I hope you're right,' Harry muttered. 'As
soon as the scan's done she'll be admitted to
the paediatric ward. Kathryn Cross has been
alerted and is on her way in.'

Some relief filtered into the muddle in Noah's
head. 'I hear she's good.'

'Better than good. Her reputation's stellar.'

'Glad she's on Holly's side then.' A bed was
being rolled along towards them. 'This for
Holly?'

Harry glanced around. 'Stacey, the porter's
here to take Holly to Radiology. You go with
her, and then on to the paediatric ward and a
family room.'

The look Stacey gave the poor man said no
one would've been able to stop her. 'My family
will come, too.' No question about that either.
Then she looked to him, a query in her face.

'You want me there?' Noah asked. He still

had to tell her what Harry had said regarding Holly's injuries.

'Yes.' She looked away, and back at him, a stricken expression on her face. 'Sorry. You do whatever suits you. I'm going with Holly. But…' She swallowed and nodded. 'I'd like you to stay around with us.'

'I'll be waiting outside Radiology.' He had no idea why this was important to him. He wasn't even going to start trying to figure it out. Chances were he'd be wrong. Stacey telling Harry to talk to him had made him a part of this family's problem, their fears, and he wanted to be there with them. Especially for Stacey.

Just like that he felt he belonged, if only for a few hours, and it gave him a deep sense of homecoming. Which was absurd. He didn't know these people, and one look at Stacey and Holly and deep inside there was a softening of the hopelessness he'd known most of his life, a sense of finally finding what he'd been looking for. From the moment he'd walked up to her on the dance floor there'd been a connection he'd never found before, a connection that simply wasn't going away.

One night had been all it had taken to mark him for ever. She'd been generous in her love-making, fun and open, and so damned special it was a constant ache in his heart.

Now she was on the other side of the door into Radiology with her heart breaking as she watched over her little girl fighting to regain consciousness. Anastasia was a mother. It didn't change how he felt about her. He only wished he'd known sooner.

What difference would that have made?

He would've still reacted the same way to seeing her that first morning on the ward. He'd still have smelt citrus perfume, been drawn in by her beautiful face, known how those curves felt on his palms.

Some things couldn't be changed. Best he accept it and get on with supporting Anastasia as much as she let him.

Had she got on with her life in the way she'd expected when she'd thanked him that night? Had she known she was pregnant and having sex with him, a complete stranger, as a way of accepting her condition and moving forward? Had he been a part of her decision over a man she had been about to commit to? She'd said she was single, and so far no one but her family had turned up here to be with Holly.

A lot of questions with no answers whirled around his mind. If there ever was a time for that. There must be. Despite today's bombshell, she was becoming more important to him all the time, and they'd spent little of that together.

It was that connection working between them. Inexplicable, yet it was there, distracting him from his long-held belief that love like his parents had had was rare, and probably not for him.

'Why don't you join Stacey?' Her father stood in front of him.

Noah got to his feet. 'I'll wait a bit, let you all spend time with Holly. It must've been a hell of a shock when she was hit by that skateboarder.' But he wanted to be with Stacey more than anything.

Ian studied him for a long moment. 'It was. She's so tiny and defenceless. Stacey adores her and nothing's going to come between them.' It sounded like a warning.

'From the little I know of Anastasia, I'm sure you're right.'

I know I care about her too much, and that I want to know more, want to further our relationship.

So why was her father looking at him as though summing him up? Wary of any man Anastasia might be interested in? Or just him? They were a tight family, but surely that didn't mean she was off limits? 'Make that, I know you're right. She's very straightforward in pursuing what she wants. It's one of the things I like about her.' Not that he could think of anything he didn't like.

Ian relaxed. 'It's what makes her such a good mother.'

Noah couldn't say why, but he felt he'd been accepted. Neither did he understand if that was important to him, or to Anastasia. But he'd run with it and see where it led. 'It's also why she's a superb nurse.'

'Come on.' Her father headed back into the small room, not looking to see if he followed.

Noah quietly followed and scoped the scene from the doorway. His heart went out to the little girl under the sheet, and to her mother holding her hand and watching over her with a look that said no one, nothing, was going to hurt Holly any more than she already had been. Stacey was tough and soft; loving beyond reason. Noah's heart swelled, filling with an emotion he was afraid to name.

CHAPTER SIX

STACEY SAT IN a chair at the bedside, her arm through the bars keeping Holly from rolling out if—when she woke up. Because she was going to come round. There was no alternative. Her baby would get through this. *They* would get through this. What had the radiology technician said? She looked around the room, locked eyes with Noah. 'Holly's going to be all right, isn't she?'

'Yes.'

He could've said a lot of medical stuff, talked in jargon that normally she'd understand but not today without having to put a lot of effort into thinking. Obviously he understood because all he'd said was, 'Yes.' She wanted to cry. Wanted, and very nearly did. But she wouldn't cry in front of Holly, not even when her girl wouldn't notice. She was the mother. The strong adult in this partnership. Holly was not going to see her wailing and carrying on. So she sniffed, and dug deep for a smile. 'Thanks for that.'

'You're welcome.'

'Noah?' Unbeknown to Noah, he was the strong person in their relationship, whatever that was. She had to tell him. This was not the time to be avoiding the truth. Wiping her eyes with a handful of tissues, she drew a breath. But not while her family were here.

'Yes?' he asked.

She thought about what to say, staring at him, believing in him, and yet worried. He might cry for their daughter and be pleased to know he was Holly's dad. He might swear and accuse her of fabricating his fatherhood for her gain. There were a hundred things he might do and say. She wasn't ready. She had to be. 'Nothing.'

'You sure?'

Not at all. 'I need to talk to you.' She pulled another tissue from the box and blew noisily.

Her mother was watching them from the other side of Holly's bed. 'Noah, we'll give you and Stacey time together, but first can you tell us what the scan means? Apart from Holly is going to be all right. How all right? No lasting damage? Or will there be ongoing problems?'

Her parents hadn't ignored Noah, had taken to him as she'd hoped. Almost. There was still a seed of doubt that would probably last until he'd been told about Holly and they all knew if he accepted her. 'Do you mind explaining, Noah?' Stacey asked, giving him permission to talk about her daughter to her family.

'Sure.' He gave a brief outline of what had shown up on the brain scan and the X-ray of Holly's arm. 'Basically it all comes down to a concussion that the doctors want to keep an eye on over the next twenty-four hours at least. Her arm's broken, hence the cast. I can tell you that with very young children it doesn't take long for a fracture to heal. Holly has been lucky.'

'Luckier still if it hadn't happened,' Stacey's father said.

Knowing how her father felt about the accident that had caused him to lose a foot, Stacey knew he was aching for Holly. Now that she'd calmed down and felt some relief at what Noah told them, she quietly admonished her father. 'Dad, you never wanted Toby or me to grow up not living life to the full and getting the odd knock. I feel the same about Holly, though I admit I wasn't going as far as thinking a run-in with a skateboard would make her tougher.'

Toby grinned. 'Like me falling out of the tree in the back garden and breaking both my arms when you said I shouldn't climb it.' Dad had cried that day, and Toby had survived, no less adventurous afterwards when it came to having fun. 'Or that time Stacey got up on the roof to get the tennis ball out of the gutter.' He looked at Noah. 'Our house is three storeys high.'

'I'm not surprised. She likes pushing the boundaries.'

Suddenly her mother looked at Stacey, her eyes full of meaning. 'We'll go and get something to eat, leave you for a while.' She was saying spend time alone with *Noah* and Holly. No pressure. But if she didn't tell him now, when did she? Was there such a thing as the perfect opportunity? What if something worse had happened to Holly and he hadn't known? Gulp. Now the threatening tears were too close for comfort.

'Okay.'

Bending over the bed, her mother kissed Holly on both cheeks. 'See you later, sweet pea. Get better for Grannie, for all of us.'

The tears were filling Stacey's eyes and she had to look away, still holding Holly's hand. They'd been so lucky, but it was hard to accept when her girl wasn't opening her eyes or giggling and asking for an ice cream. 'Thanks, Mum.'

'You need time without all of us hanging around.' Her meaning was so clear it was a wonder Noah didn't get the message. Talk to Noah. Tell him the truth. Did that mean Mum approved of him? Or just wanted the obstacle gone from the room?

Gulp. 'Can you get me some basic toiletries from the supermarket? I'm staying overnight.'

'Already on my list.' Mum came around to hug her. 'Tell her we love her the moment she opens her eyes.' Sniff.

'You bet.' Sniff. She hugged back. 'Love you, too.' Her family was always there for each other. When Dad had been injured they'd made sure he didn't get down or let the loss of a foot change him for ever. She'd been the one to harangue him into walking on crutches every day, more times than he thought he should. She'd been the person to get him outside for the first time on his prosthetic foot to visit his friends at the pub for a pint and try to get back to normal. Her parents had always supported her from the moment she'd told them she was pregnant. For her, this was what family meant. Not everyone was so lucky.

Her father gave her a special dad hug that always warmed her, no matter how upset she might be. 'Take care. Watch over her for all of us.'

They wouldn't be able to stay away that long. 'I will.' Then she turned to Toby and wound her arms around him. 'Don't beat yourself up. It wasn't your fault.'

'Bossy boots.' But he gave her a small smile.

'Someone has to be.' She smiled, then returned to sit with her girl. 'Hey, Holly, it's Mummy. How're you doing, little one? Can you wake up now?' It didn't matter what the doctors said, she needed Holly to open her eyes before she'd feel totally at ease. Her cheeks were colourless, and never had she been so still. Or quiet. Usually hyperactive, this was unreal. She was a right little giggler so to be silent came out of left field. 'Talk to Mummy, sweetheart.'

'Here, get this into you.' Noah held out a paper cup of coffee. 'Not the best, but it's something.' He pulled up the other chair and sat down beside her, another full cup in his hand. 'How are you doing? Feel any better now that you know there's no brain damage?'

'Definitely.' She soaked in the sight of Holly, barely able to breathe. 'She's so little and breakable, I can't believe how lucky we've been. But concussion's no fun, and she's only two. I've seen other children suffering from it, and thought how awful it was, but this is my daughter. I can't quite comprehend it, and yet I can. I know the details, the whys and what-ifs. A part of me is terrified that they've got it wrong and she's not going to recover quickly.'

'She will.'

'How can you be so positive?' She *was* over-reacting, but that was the mother in her.

'The scan's normal. Besides, it's what I want. Not a very medical answer, I know, but it's how I feel.'

Stacey stared at him. Had he guessed the truth? Nothing showed in his expression to suggest so. Did she know what she was looking for? He'd hide it, wouldn't he? He could be waiting for her to fess up.

'For both you and Holly,' he added.

'Oh, Noah.' If only he knew. Well, he would, if she found the courage to tell him.

A murmur came from the bed.

Stacey spun around and leapt up to lean over the sidebar. 'Holly? It's Mummy, sweetheart.'

'Mmm.'

Reaching out, Stacey touched her cheek with the backs of her fingers. 'Holly. I'm here.'

'Mummy.' Her eyes fluttered open, then closed again.

Relief poured into Stacey and the tears flowed freely. So much for not letting Holly see. 'Holly, you're in bed and Mummy's with you.' Now she was talking gibberish.

Holly was looking at her, confusion filling her beautiful grey eyes. Her father's eyes.

Handing her cup to Noah, Stacey dropped the bar and sat on the bed, reaching for her girl, carefully slipping under her and holding her against her breast. 'There, sweetheart. Mummy's got you.'

'She looks like you,' Noah said quietly.

'So people tell me.'

Don't look at her eyes.

'You don't agree?'

'Yes, I can see quite a few Wainwright genes in there.' She'd spent most of Holly's life looking for signs of Noah, and so far only her eyes came close. 'She's a happy wee soul, always giggling and having fun.'

'Like her mum.'

Deep breath. 'Noah. I need to tell you something.' She couldn't put it off for another moment. This was eating her up. Now or never. Never wasn't an option. She didn't want to do that to Holly or Noah. They were bonded through Holly, and watch out anyone or anything that threatened to come between them.

Heavy grey eyes locked onto her, not moving, not looking at the girl who was his daughter. 'This sounds serious.'

'It is.'

Please, still like me when I've finished.

'Holly's a little over two years old.'

'I heard you tell the woman her date of birth when we arrived here.' The words were spoken in a monotone, as though he was holding back an emotion she wouldn't like. Or he was afraid of? His mouth flattened. His shoulders were tightening, and his eyes boring into her. Getting the idea?

'That's right. Nine months give a day or three after the dance.' Her chest rose, then she spilled the facts before she could overthink this. 'Holly was conceived the night we were together.'

He didn't blink. Didn't move at all. His mouth was still flat, as though he'd been expecting news he didn't want to hear. The grey stare darkened, not giving away anything her words might've wrought on him, but coffee spilled onto the floor between his feet from the squashed cardboard mug in his hand.

She was his focus, a long, breath-defying stare. Her stomach curled into a tight little ball, her heart slowed while her lungs struggled to do their job. 'It's true, Noah. Holly is your daughter.'

At last his gaze moved slowly down to the precious bundle tucked against her, focusing on his daughter. Stacey held Holly tighter, closer. She preferred it when he looked at her with all those blistering questions and not at Holly. Holly was innocent. So was she. She hadn't planned on getting pregnant. It had just happened.

This beautiful child was her daughter. Noah's daughter, too, but hers no matter what. He had a choice—accept or deny. She'd never had a choice, and had never wanted one. From the moment she'd learned she was pregnant there hadn't been a single doubt she'd love her baby and was to raise him or her no matter what the world threw at them. Noah would accept eventually. He would. But then what? Would he want to know his daughter, love her, support her? Or deposit money into a bank account every month and leave it at that?

No, she could not believe Noah would do that. He was honourable. But this was about more than that. It was about responsibility, about caring and sharing, about wanting to be a father, about love. Her heart banged. Love. Was Noah ready for that? She'd often wondered if he would ever love her. Now she needed to know, more than anything, would he love Holly?

'I used protection,' he intoned in that same voice.

'I know.' Condoms every time. But Holly was real.

'You're saying they didn't all work?' A scathing tone.

'It's the only answer I've been able to come up with throughout the years since.' Okay, so she could do scathing, too.

Silence took over, only interrupted by voices as people passed the open door. Stacey glanced down at Holly, and felt her heart drop. Was she asleep now? Or had she fallen unconscious again? Her fingers found a pulse in Holly's neck. Using her phone, she timed it and sighed with relief. All good. Brushing a kiss on her daughter's forehead, she glanced up at Noah.

He was watching them both intently.

'Noah?'

He said nothing, letting the silence expand. This time a little chilly.

She opted for quiet, letting Noah absorb what she'd told him. No doubt he'd be doing the sums to make sure she hadn't lied. Her back stiffened. Lying wasn't one of her habits. But, then, how often had he been told he was the father of a two-year-old girl?

'Is it true you weren't in a relationship when we got together at the dance? That you hadn't had an argument with your partner?'

'I was single and had been for a year. There was no one else. Holly is yours, Noah. You are her father.' Her mouth dried. She'd known there'd be questions, lots of them. But how to cope with them without sounding needy and pathetic?

He locked his steady gaze on her, watched her for a long, long moment.

Her breath stuck in her chest as she waited.

His knuckles were white against his hips,

his body rigid, chin thrust forward. Then he slumped. 'I believe you.'

The air exhaled from Stacey's lungs in a rush. 'Thank you,' she whispered.

'Who'd have thought? I used protection.' He shook his head. 'Each time.'

'I remember.' Tears poured down her cheeks and she did nothing to stop them. 'I tried to find you, but I had little to go on. Noah—that was it. I didn't even know you were a doctor.' She hadn't told anyone why she wanted to find the man she'd danced with. Certainly hadn't mentioned spending the rest of the night in his hotel room having sex. And how she'd been reluctant to leave next morning but knowing she had to. They hadn't had a future.

Noah had been heading away somewhere unknown, and she had been getting on with a new job at London Riverside while trying to get over a broken heart. 'I wanted you to know about Holly. I really did.' Her heart was cracking for them all. Now Noah finally knew, she understood she never wanted to lose him. She felt deeply for him and wanted a future with him.

He was watching her, his chest rising and falling as he breathed deep and often. Then his eyes drifted down to Holly in her arms. His chest rose, stalled. His eyes softened while his hands gripped his hips tighter. His tongue slid over his lip from left to right. 'You've had to cope on your own. That must've been hard.'

'My family supports me. But, yes, there have been times when I've longed for you to be around, to be in Holly's life.'

If not mine.

'It would've changed so many things. She needs you as much as she needs me.'

'So why didn't you tell me the day we bumped into each other?' Wariness was creeping into his face.

'On the ward, surrounded with patients and staff? In the tearoom when at any moment we'd get interrupted?'

'Come on, Stacey. You can do better than that.' It was a comment, not an accusation.

But he was right. 'True. I'm sorry. After looking for you so long, when the moment arrived I was stunned. Suddenly Holly wasn't just mine for real. Then when we had coffee that night it was too noisy, and then, well, we kissed and went to your house and you know what happened.'

His gaze fell onto Holly, almost though he was sucking in the sight of *his* girl. When he spoke it was quietly, as though afraid to disturb his daughter. 'I sort of understand, but there was afterwards, and the morning over breakfast, and any number of times.'

'I felt guilty for getting distracted. I planned on telling you today. I really did.' Thud, thud went her heart.

Lifting his head slowly, dragging his eyes around to her, he stared at her again. 'I guess it must've been difficult, not really knowing me that well. But now I do know, there's a lot to absorb.' Then he turned away and strode out of the room without another word.

Leaving her feeling bereft. And fully aware that she was very close to being in love with him.

When that had happened, she wasn't sure. It wasn't as though there'd been much time for falling in love. Maybe it didn't take long when it was the real deal. It could've happened three years ago when he'd danced with her. Or held her in his arms as they'd made love that same night. Or on Monday when he'd turned and she'd seen him for the first time since that wonderful time. Or today when he'd leapt to help when she'd received the dreadful news about Holly's accident. Or could be that now she'd finally been able to get the truth out to him she'd let other emotions to the fore.

Holly. This had to be about her more than her own feelings for Noah. Loving him, rightly or wrongly, could not dominate the coming days when they sorted out where they went from here.

Give Noah time to think it all through. Don't hassle him. Nothing to be gained by doing that. Concentrate on seeing Holly through her injuries and getting back on her little feet.

That was her role. Be her mother first and second. Nothing else mattered.

Tell that to her newly awakened heart. And Noah. She gazed down at the greatest gift she'd ever received.

Thank you for believing me, Noah. Now, please, come back and talk to me.

It had hurt beyond imagination when Angus had walked away from her after a lifetime together as friends then lovers. His betrayal had undermined her capacity to love without question. Not that she'd tried.

Then along had come Noah, followed by Holly. She wanted to give the same back. Share the gift of their daughter. She'd never stop doing the absolute best for their daughter either, surrounding her with love and care and encouragement. She also wanted to love Noah openly, be loved in return.

Her heart lurched. That was unlikely. Noah had been friendly, even aware of her as more than a nurse or friend, but for him to love her seemed a long way off, if ever possible. He'd not said as much, but he'd been hurt by his ex, and that would carry over to any relationship he had. Which only said there wasn't much opportunity for her to win his heart.

Noah strode along the side of the road, head down, hands jammed in his pockets. The air was chilly, more rain due any minute. People were walking past him in all directions, intent on getting inside before the weather dumped on them.

'I'm a father.'

If Anastasia was being honest with him. Why wouldn't she be? There was nothing for her to gain, because he knew those tricks, though not even Christine had been cold enough to throw a baby into the mix, only her plans for two. Was Anastasia that calculating? Had seeing his home been the catalyst? It didn't seem right. She'd asked to see him today, and now he thought maybe it had been to tell him about Holly.

Hearing she had a daughter had slammed into him. Why, when he hadn't been a part of her life except for one night, had it knocked him sideways? She was entitled to a life of her own. He had no claims on her. Even if Holly wasn't his, Stacey didn't owe it to him to mention the child unless they got into a relationship.

To be told the child was his had taken the

ground out from under him. It was a game-changer. He didn't know what to think. What should he do? What did he want to do? Accept Holly as his, accept Stacey had told the truth without checking it out? Huh, a part of him already did, or wanted to at least.

Holly was gorgeous, even unconscious and as pale as whitewash. Biased already? She was so tiny, as two-year-olds were. When her eyes had fluttered open he'd felt a tap on his heart, and that had been before he'd known who she'd inherited those from.

Sounds like you're truly believing she's yours.

Could he be? Did he want to be a father? He'd always thought he would have children one day. But he'd expected to be there from the beginning, not come in a couple of years on. Stacey said she'd done all she could to find him, and thinking back he really had to believe that. There was no way she could've found him in Auckland. He'd never worked at London General so no one at the dance had known him except for the friend who'd dragged him along to keep him company until he got up the courage to ask the light of his life for a dance.

He shivered as rain got under the collar of his jacket and trickled down his back. What did Anastasia expect of him now? Did she want a permanent relationship? Or financial gain?

Or—and this was what he'd want if he was going to accept Holly as his own—did she just hope he'd be a father to their daughter? That would suit him. He could love Holly unconditionally. He wouldn't be looking for love, he'd be giving it wholeheartedly with no expectations of what he'd get back.

Wasn't that how all love was meant to be? Wasn't that how his parents had loved him, and he them in return? And each other. So why wasn't he listening to his heart and giving everything to Anastasia? Because he was afraid she'd be another Christine.

Come on, she's not.

Stacey was strong, independent despite living with her family, and open to others. Her family supported her, and no doubt did a lot for Holly, but she gave it back just as much, if not more. The little she'd told him about her father's accident and how she'd stepped up showed that. Holly wouldn't miss out on what was important in life. But *he* might. It was him who could blow this tentative relationship apart by not trusting Anastasia fully, by letting the past get in the way of the present and future. Stacey and Holly were his future, if he'd let them.

Noah stumbled. A new shock registered in his beleaguered mind. He was accepting Holly was his? Already? Without thinking about everything involved? Without proof? Couldn't be. Sure, he was coming close to falling deeply for Anastasia, but that didn't mean stepping up and taking responsibility for her daughter, no questions asked.

Her father had agreed she was straightforward about everything. Her father. So this was why Ian had been eyeing him so intently. Her family knew he was their granddaughter's father. Were they expecting him to find out today? It made sense when he thought about it, explained a lot of things. If he chose to believe Anastasia. Why shouldn't he? Not everyone was out to get what they could from him.

'Look out.' Someone grabbed his arm as he was about to step off the footpath and cross the road, right in the path of an oncoming car. 'Thanks,' he muttered, and waited impatiently for the lights to change. Getting taken out by a car wouldn't help anyone, especially Anastasia when she was already distressed about Holly, and waiting for his next move.

Holly. What a cute little girl. She had her mother's looks and her thick hair might be curly but it was the same dark blonde. Was he really her father? And if so, what was he going to do about it?

As the first spots of rain touched down on his face, Noah ducked into a pub and ordered a whisky. 'A large one.' He headed to a table by a window and sat, rolling the glass back and forth between his hands.

Only that morning he'd been impatient to see Anastasia, arriving at the tube station early. The moment she'd stepped into his view he'd felt deep happiness. His stomach had softened, his heart had thumped.

The happiness was still there, if only he'd let it grow and stop trying to push it away. He'd always wanted to fall in love and experience the wonder of having someone who loved him back and supported him. But he'd also always been afraid of screwing up again. He hadn't fallen deeply enough in love with Christine, but enough to believe they could make a go of it, and hopefully get to where his parents had been. He'd been wrong. Unfair to Christine even. While she'd been out for everything she could get from him, a clinical relationship like his aunt and uncle had, he'd been blind in his bid to get what he'd wanted.

How he'd not recognised that from the outset had always bothered him and made him even more cautious. He had made a big mistake in thinking that love could grow if both people involved put the effort in.

Love happened. From what he'd seen with friends it seemed to be there from the get-go, like a light switch being flicked on, and not necessarily with the kind of person anyone expected. Then he'd met Anastasia and within hours—or had it been minutes on the dance floor?—every idea of the perfect partner had gone in a puff of need.

Could be Anastasia was the perfect woman for him. Might not be either. How did a man decide? He could go with his heart. Or let his brain choose.

Or he could just go back to the hospital and sit with Anastasia and his daughter, and absorb the sense of them, their loving natures and generous hearts.

A bitter laugh huffed from his mouth. How could he think that about Holly when he'd only seen her unconscious? What about that small smile and the word 'Mummy' whispering across her lips? Not so out of it then. And that's why he felt she was just like her mother. How could she not be?

Sipping his whisky, he stared out the window into the night lit by streetlamps. Rain slapped the pavement, glistening in the light. It was cosy in here, yet he shivered. He was teetering on a cliff edge. He wanted to grab Anastasia and Holly, hold them to him for ever and make the most of everything. He wanted to go back to early that morning when he had been climbing out of bed and heading to the bathroom for a shave, and when he hadn't known about this child who'd turned the world as he knew it upside down.

Hell, he didn't know what he wanted—except not to make a bigger mess of everything than it already was.

It's only a mess because you're overthinking everything.

He wanted to get this right. For Holly. For Anastasia and, yes, for himself. Then 'how' was the next big question. That had to be decided by talking to Anastasia, not just to himself.

There was a warmth in his gut and touching his heart. If it was true and Holly was his, he'd become a father in the time it had taken Anastasia to say, 'Holly was conceived the night we were together. It's true, Noah. Holly is your daughter.' No planning, no nine months to get used to the idea, no agreeing it was a good thing to start a family when he wasn't in a relationship. A matter of seconds and he'd become a father. Whether he'd wanted to or not.

He could walk away. Except he'd never do that. He knew the pain of losing parents, the pain of not being taken in by other family to share their love and camaraderie. It wasn't something he'd ever impose on his daughter. Holly would be well cared for and loved by the

Wainwright family and have everything important to grow up into a wonderful woman.

Could he do any better? Did he want to? Yes, damn it, he did. She would be loved by him as well, with all that entailed. But to trust Anastasia completely was a big ask. Despite her reassurances about being happy with her lot, she might change when she fully understood his background and all that was on offer.

Another sip of his drink and he thought about Christine. His wife had hurt him, but she hadn't wrecked him. She'd let him down by not meeting his love with hers. He'd wanted a family, like the one he'd known for the first ten years of his life. She'd never had that herself so didn't believe in it.

Anastasia came from a loving environment and gave love out without thought. Love was a part of her. Did she have any for him?

His head was going round and round, and getting nowhere. Shoving the almost full glass aside, he straightened up and headed for the door and the wet weather. He was not making any decisions about any damned thing tonight. He was going back to the hospital to sit with Anastasia and Holly, watching over them as they waited out the time it took for Holly to get well enough to go home.

CHAPTER SEVEN

STACEY OPENED HER eyes slowly and looked around the darkened room from the bed she was sprawled over. Shock rippled through her at the man standing at the end of Holly's bed, hands in pockets, a poignant look on his face as he gazed down at his daughter. 'Noah?' she whispered.

Slowly he turned to face her, sadness radiating out at her. 'How hard *did* you try to find me?'

He was regretting missing out on the early years of Holly's life. 'On the train heading home that morning I wished I'd taken a moment to ask when you were coming back from wherever it was you were headed. I didn't know if you were going on holiday or off to a permanent job in Britain or another country.

'You mentioned staying at the hotel since you'd packed up your house so your move seemed long term. I wanted to see you again.'

She paused, hoping for a response, got none. 'At work on Monday I asked my friends to check around at London General to see if anyone knew you and they came up blank. Most people didn't even know me, let alone who I was dancing with.'

Another pause while she thought back to those frantic days when she'd almost begged people to give her a name for the man no one had known. 'Now I know you'd never worked at London General it makes sense.'

'And that was it?'

'No. A few weeks later I found I was pregnant. At first it was scary. I was single, still getting over my broken relationship.' Tell him how he'd made Angus start sliding into the background? Maybe not. Noah didn't look as though he'd want to hear that. 'But as the days turned to weeks I began to get excited. I was going to be a mother, and even if I had to raise my child on my own, it was wonderful.'

'So you gave up looking for me?'

Her chest ached for him. And her. She'd told him this already. He was looking for reasons to be angry with her while he accepted the truth in front of him. 'No, Noah, I didn't. I began a methodical search of the hospital, checking out all the medical staff, and then anyone else working there who might've known you. You didn't exist. That was the only blight on my pregnancy. Like I said before, I never stopped looking for you.'

Lifting her hands and turning them palms upwards, she asked, 'What else was I supposed to do? There's more than one Noah out there, believe me.' And none that she'd seen were a patch on this one.

To give him his due, he was trying to deal with the situation in a cautious but non-aggressive way. No surprise really. She'd shocked the living daylights out of him, and that would take time to absorb and decide how he'd deal with Holly. And her. He'd probably never felt more for her than like and care, which wasn't enough. He wouldn't've been stupid enough to fall for her in a few hours when they'd been making love. For him that had probably been sex, not making love, and he'd got as much as he could. Sex that they'd repeated already this week. Sex that to her was making love and made her feel happy. 'You said you only tried once to find me.'

'I don't think that's important right now, Anastasia.'

Sudden anger burst from her. 'Anastasia. What's with not using Stacey like everyone else, huh?' She'd liked how he'd used her full name, but tonight it made her feel he was putting her in a bubble, to be looked at and thought about without the hindrance of others who knew and loved her.

'Stacey it is, then. Not that it changes a thing. We have a problem, and I'm trying to understand it all. Starting with the fact that three years have gone by when I didn't know you'd become pregnant. *Allegedly* with *my* child.' Noah glared at her, then sighed. 'Sorry, that doesn't help. I owe you better than that.'

Swallowing her own anger, she nodded. 'It's okay. Really. I expected denial in the beginning.' And withdrawal. Even disinterest. Though, no, not that. She'd watched Noah gazing at Holly earlier with something like hope and a tentative love growing in his eyes. Maybe he wasn't aware of those emotions, but they'd been there, she'd swear. 'I'm not going to make a scene, Noah. Holly's yours. There was no one else in my life at the time. Not even another one-night stand,' she added with unexpected bitterness. So much for not making a scene.

Getting off the chair, she crossed to her girl, and reached over the guard rail to touch her. To make sure she was real. To feel that soft skin and the warmth that was Holly inside and out. 'Love you, baby,' she whispered.

Your father is the only man I ever slept with for one night.

He was still the only man other than Angus,

and he'd made a greater impact in one night than Angus had in a lifetime. She'd loved Angus, but after Noah she'd realised how much of her relationship with Angus had been about friendship. She'd loved him, totally, with all she had to offer. It just hadn't held the passion she'd found with Noah. Passion that still woke her, that had begun twisting her heart every time she saw him, whether at work, in the street, or here when he was struggling to trust her honesty.

Standing at the end of the bed, Noah said nothing, but she could feel his eyes boring into her. Looking for what? Warning signs that said she was a liar? That she was looking for any man to be her daughter's father? That she'd use him to get what she wanted?

The anger was back, increasing as though it had been waiting for months, if not years, for this moment to express itself. Anger over not being able to find Noah. Over not having told him who she was apart from Anastasia, which no one would have recognised as her name. Over having a child and not being able to tell her who her father was and why he wasn't around. Whipping around, she snapped in a low voice, 'Go away. Leave us alone. I don't want toxic vibes to disturb Holly. She doesn't need anything but love at the moment.'

Steely grey eyes locked on her.

She waited, cool on the outside, seething internally. He didn't believe anything she said. He was going to walk away. From his daughter. Maybe for the time it took to get his head around the fact he was a parent, like it or not. He hadn't had enough time to think it all through, yet he was going to leave. She sensed it in his stance, in those eyes and the grim tightness of his usually kind mouth. Not knowing what to say to change his mind, she waited, and waited.

'Mummy.'

Stacey's shoulders drooped forward, her knees softened, and her heart rate increased. Gripping the rail, she turned to her daughter. 'Hey, baby, Mummy's here.' She dropped the rail and sank onto the bed to lift Holly into her arms, and lay her chin on her head, breathed deeply to absorb her girl's smell. Noah could go do whatever he liked. So long as he didn't upset Holly.

'That went well,' Noah muttered as he stood in the lift taking him to the bottom level and his car outside after talking to a nurse about Holly's condition since Anastasia hadn't taken back her permission for him to ask the staff.

He'd been going to sit with An—with Stacey and Holly while he thought about his new life. It *was* new. If nothing else, he was now a father. He wouldn't be a remote dad, only turning up for birthdays and Christmas, adding to Stacey's bank account to make sure Holly never went without.

So he did believe the child was his? Actually… He sighed. He did. Holly's eyes were replicas of those he saw in the mirror every morning while shaving. The truth was in her mother's voice, face, stance. Stacey hadn't lied. Holly was his daughter. Hadn't he admitted that to himself already? He should've told Stacey. Instead, he'd pushed her hard about how she hadn't found him when he'd known the odds had been stacked against them from the beginning. He tipped his head back to stare at the lift ceiling. He wasn't playing fair. Being blindsided was not an excuse. He was human?

So is Anastasia. Stacey.

He'd been looking for hidden meanings behind her reactions, and had got an earful of disappointment in him instead. Which only showed she was the woman he hoped, and not one who lied to get what she wanted.

The lift jerked to a halt and the doors slid open. Two women in nurses' uniforms joined him, one pressing the button for the third floor.

He made a decision. Reaching around the nurse, he pressed four—Paediatrics. And Stacey.

In the ward he found a nurse to ask if he could

use their kitchen to make a coffee for Stacey and was told yes, and to take her a piece of the fruit cake on the bench.

'Here, thought you might want something to drink.' He placed the mug and plate with cake on the table beside her. 'You haven't eaten at all.'

'Mum brought me some sandwiches earlier, but I'm not hungry.' She was sitting with her knees under her chin and her arms wound tightly around her legs.

'Try something.' When he'd walked in she'd been watching Holly with such tenderness it had torn his heart in two. He knew that look from his childhood. It meant everything to him, then and now. Holly didn't know how lucky she was. He pulled up the chair and sat down. 'I'm sorry for being a prat.' He wasn't going to come out with things like he was still in shock, no matter how true they were. Excuses didn't solve any of what lay between them.

Her gaze still on Holly, she shrugged. 'It's all right.'

It wasn't. There was hurt in her voice, put there by him. 'She's doing fine, Stacey.' Noah sat back quietly and watched the two females dominating his life as though he was guarding them, which he was in a way, though what from was another question with no answer.

'Sure.' Finally Stacey stretched her legs out,

and reached for the mug. 'Thanks for this. I wanted a coffee but couldn't bear to leave Holly even for a few minutes. She might wake and panic if I'm not here.'

'Your parents have gone home?'

'Yes. They didn't want to, but I insisted.'

'You're all so close.'

Finally she looked at him. 'Yes, we are. Always have been.'

And I'd be a fool to forget that.

'Feel free to ask me anything you need to know to make this real,' she added, then she went back to watching over her daughter.

And he went back to watching over them both, with a lot of questions making themselves known in his head.

Stacey yawned and leaned back, closing her eyes.

Noah fought the urge to go across and kiss her cheek. Instead, he stood to gaze down at the beautiful girl lying in the bed attached to the monitor on the stand behind her. A weight settled over his heart. Not a painful one but sadness for the two years of her life he'd missed. He hadn't been there to hold her when she'd arrived in the world, hadn't kissed her or promised to love and care for her for the rest of his life. Hadn't heard her first word or seen her first steps. Her giggles didn't ring in his skull. He didn't know what her favourite food was, if she slept all night or woke on and off.

'Her favourite toy is Goggy, a well-worn teddy bear that has to go to bed with her every night or there's hell to pay. Mum's bringing Goggy in with her tomorrow.'

Noah smiled. 'Goggy, eh?'

'There's a doll named Jack after her best friend at day care.'

He laughed. 'Does Jack know that?'

'Yes, but I don't think he realises what it means or their friendship might be off.' Stacey sat up straighter.

Noah turned to look at Stacey. For the first time since they'd caught up no reminiscing smile came his way. But at least she continued giving him snippets about their girl. 'Holly loves butterflies and frogs, hates cornflakes and eggs.'

Returning to his chair, he waited for more as the heaviness inside him lightened.

'I can push her on the swing for half an hour and it's nowhere near long enough. Brushing her hair is an ordeal for everyone. Though a couple of months ago she found the kitchen scissors and cut off large hunks.' Stacey's mouth twisted into a cute smile filled with reverence for Holly. 'She's a little minx. Uncle Toby is fair game for having his clothes hidden in the same place behind the couch every day, while Granddad is a sucker for cuddles and sweets whenever I'm not looking. Grandma is the kiss-it-better go-to when I'm not around.'

'It must be hard going off to work every day, not knowing what you might miss.'

'It is.'

'Is Holly the reason you asked to spend time with me today?'

Her eyes met his. 'Yes. I was going to tell you about her.'

Convenient. Or truthful. Judging by that steady look she was giving him, definitely truthful. 'I see.'

'I don't think you do, Noah. When I saw you on Monday for the first time since all this started, I've known what I had to do, and that there was no reason to wait. As it wasn't something to say at work or in a noisy café I thought meeting up at the weekend would be best.'

'True. But—'

Her hand was up. 'Stop right there. I always intended telling you. I don't have the right to decide if Holly knows her father or not.' She breathed in. 'I was nervous, to say the least.' Shaking her head, her lips curved into a small wry smile. 'Here, with Holly injured and floating in and out of consciousness, I wanted you to learn your relationship to her so you could be here for her.' Stray tears slipped down her cheeks and she brushed them away angrily.

It would be too easy to go to her, lift her into his arms and kiss away the distress darkening those beautiful eyes. He wanted to make her smile, and be happy again, and take away all her fears—especially those concerning him and what he wanted for the future with Holly. He wasn't ready for that.

There was a lot to consider. Especially Anastasia and his feelings for her. He had to get everything right, not make half-baked decisions they might all regret later. Putting the past away for ever was proving difficult now he was faced with taking a giant step forward without any guarantees it would work out.

'Tell me about your family.' Her words cut through his turmoil.

'Which one? My devoted, loving parents I still miss? Or my aunt and uncle who believe life is about being aloof and proper, and not falling head over heels in love, like my father did? According to Robert, if Dad hadn't married Mum he'd still be here. It was her love of life and friends and family that had them on that road the night they were killed.'

He sounded bitter, because he still was whenever he saw friends falling in love and being so happy. Now Anastasia wound him up with

hope, something he wasn't certain if she recip-
rocated even in the smallest way. Yet whenever
they touched, they fell together, no hesitation
on her part.

'You have a cousin in Auckland?'

'His mother is my mother's sister. Another
happy soul.'

Stacey was watching him, a small smile light-
ening her face for the first time in hours.

'What?'

'You've got it in you to be like that too.'

Surprise hit. 'You think?' She was right, only
he'd thought he had to find the right person to
help him bring it out. Could it be he should've
got on with being happy with his lot and let his
relatives get on with theirs? Then he said something stupid. 'I'll take you to meet Robert and
Alice next weekend. I have to sign some docu-
ments for them.' That would certainly test Stacey. Hard to be cheerful around those two, and
she'd get to see the mansion he'd spent time in
growing up. That'd tell if she suddenly thought
being rich might be a good idea.

Noah groaned. How horrid could he be? Stacey would no doubt think of all the windows
that'd need cleaning and the floors to vacuum,
rather than want to live in such a huge house.
'Stacey, I'm being a prat again. Say no if you
want to.'

She shook her head, still smiling. 'I want to know more about you, Noah. I'll come.'

Stacey slapped at her face, wiping the moisture away and probably smearing mascara over her cheeks. If there was any left after her crying jag when Holly had woken again and said, 'Mummy.' Her body ached, her heart ached more. There was a set of drums in her skull doing their best to give her a headache, and succeeding. She wanted to curl up on the bed, holding Holly close, and cuddle her all night long. Equally, she'd be afraid of holding her too tight and hurting her.

Eyes closed, Noah was sprawled in the chair. Was he asleep? Or was he going over and over the fact he was a father? He hadn't said outright she couldn't be his. Instead, he'd said he believed her, even though the doubts had crept back in since then. He had also been more willing to listen than she'd have believed. But he hadn't said a word about accepting he was a father, about what he'd want for his daughter's future, and how much time he'd want to spend with Holly. As in have her for nights, or weeks.

She'd feel bereft, not having Holly at home. A chill crept into her stomach, spread throughout her body. Could she trust Noah not to hurt her? To understand her feelings and the sense of loss just sharing Holly time between them might bring on? Of course, she was being self-ish, and had known this might happen, but she couldn't help herself. She didn't know a life without Holly in it all the time. She spoke aloud, hoping he heard.

'I put Holly before all else. I have to go to work, but she's well cared for by my family and the nursery she attends two mornings a week.' The neighbour left the gate open and that's why they were here. Would he hold that against her?

Those eyes she'd first fallen for opened and locked onto her. 'Relax, Stacey. I give you my word I will not take her away from you. You're a devoted mum and love her to bits. I've seen that already.'

She couldn't relax but some of the chill warmed. 'Thank you.' When his gaze returned to Holly she realised he hadn't made a move to hold her, or even touch her. Standing up, she crossed to the bed and lowered the rail. 'Come and sit by your daughter.'

At first she didn't think he was going to, but after a couple of laden minutes he crossed to the bed and did as instructed. Slowly he reached out and ran his finger down Holly's arm, avoid-ing the needle and tube feeding her pain relief. The look of wonder in his eyes stole Stacey's breath away. Noah was accepting his daughter.

Step one passed. Mind you, who couldn't fall for her little girl? She was so sweet and cute and downright wonderful.

A shiver ran down Stacey's spine. 'What if she'd been injured even worse than she was?'

'Don't go there. She wasn't. Be grateful for that. She's still got a little way to go before she'll be back dancing and singing, so you need to stay strong.'

He was right. The nurse in her was returning and bringing along a load of common sense. 'I wonder when she'll be able to go home.'

Noah glanced up. 'Don't rush it. Keep her here as long as possible. It's best for her.'

'I know.' Bending down, she carefully lifted Holly off the bed and placed her in her father's arms. She didn't need to tell him to be careful. 'There you go.'

As he gazed down at Holly, she moved away to sit on the chair and watch Noah falling in love. He had the right instincts, and Holly was going to be the winner. And Noah. She was glad he knew about his daughter. He'd already missed out on too much. Whatever unfolded between Noah and herself, this was the right thing to have done.

If only he could fall for her as he had for Holly. Watching his fascination with his girl, the love for Noah that'd been growing day by day came to the fore, filling her heart, making her wish she could kiss him, and hold him. Do that now and he'd think she was trying to win him over about Holly. There'd been moments between them all week whenever they had been close that had made her wonder if he felt something for her, or if he was only thinking of the sex they'd shared.

On Monday she'd wondered if she might come to love him. Today, even before this moment, she'd known deep down she was close, if not there. Only time would tell. And Noah's thoughts on the future involving the three of them.

Watching him, the tension holding her tight since the phone call to say Holly had been hurt began softening. Her neck moved without pain, her hands weren't opening and shutting into balls any more, and her toes had stopped tapping a rhythm. Her eyelids dropped, cutting off the picture mesmerising her, but it was still there inside her head as she relaxed against the back of the chair. She wasn't alone here. She had her daughter's father to share this. Very different from her parents' support. Not that she could relax entirely. They had a long way to go.

Noah's mouth dried as he gazed down at the little girl in his arms. His girl, his daughter. Holly.

Holly Wainwright. Holly Kennedy. Wham. Holly Kennedy. That was her name. No, that wasn't fair to Anastasia. But he wanted his child to carry his name. Taking a peek at Stacey, he let out a long breath. She was asleep. He could avoid that problem for now.

But it wouldn't go away unless he gave in. Like a lot of the issues they'd have to face and sit down for a full and frank discussion about. Not tonight. It was after eleven, and Stacey was shattered. She needed sleep. He'd remain here until she woke up, whatever time that was. And continue holding Holly. Unless she woke up. If she did she'd get a fright to find it wasn't Mummy holding her.

Damn, she was gorgeous, he repeated to himself. Biased, by any chance? Naturally, he smiled, and again looked at Stacey. Another gorgeous female in his life—if he was careful and didn't let her get away. She'd given him something he'd only ever dreamed of. He owed her big time. She could've kept quiet and he'd have been none the wiser, unless they'd started getting serious about each other, and he had been wishing for that—when he wasn't looking for excuses to run before he got too involved. Which proved yet again how genuine she was.

Stacey wasn't someone to ignore truth. Deep

down, he accepted that. It was what he'd been looking for, for so long.

'Hello, someone looks comfortable.' The night nurse assigned to Holly appeared at the bedside.

'Holly or Stacey?'

'Both. I'm glad Stacey's sleeping. She was exhausted.' The nurse talked in a low voice, obviously not wanting to wake anyone. 'And this little one needs all the sleep she can get.'

'It's the best cure for concussion,' Noah agreed.

'I'm going to take Holly's temperature.'

Noah remained still, holding Holly a little tighter in case she felt the ear thermometer and woke with a start.

'Temperature's normal,' the nurse commented as she read the thermometer. Then she straightened the sheets. 'I think we should put her back into bed now—so she can move her legs and good arm in her sleep,' she added as Noah tried to come up with a reason to keep holding her.

Standing, he laid his precious bundle on the bed and tucked the top sheet up to her chin. Then he leaned over and kissed her forehead. Tears filled his eyes immediately.

A box of tissues appeared in his blurred vision, and he snatched a handful. 'Thanks,' he said gruffly.

'It always gets to you, doesn't it? They're so vulnerable and you're supposed to be able to protect them from this sort of thing, but the real world's different from our hopes and dreams.'

Noah gasped as he realised this woman was presuming he was Holly's father, and had been there for her whole, short life. About to put her right, he hesitated. Why would he do that? She was a nurse on this shift and had nothing else to do with them. He was still getting his head around the fact his life had changed so completely in such a short time. Talking about it to a stranger didn't seem like a great idea. If he talked to anyone it would be to the other woman in the room. When she woke up.

CHAPTER EIGHT

'BECAUSE YOU'RE A nurse I'm letting you take Holly home later this afternoon as long as the nurses don't find a reason not to,' the paediatrician told Stacey when she did her round on Monday morning. 'She's through the worst, but you need to keep an eye on her concussion. Any sign of change and I want her back here immediately.'

'Believe me, I'll have her here fast. Can you run through everything with me one more time?' Stacey asked. 'I can't quite relax yet.'

'Medical staff make the worst caregivers of their nearest and dearest.'

'Don't they ever,' Stacey agreed. She hadn't expected to get quite so stressed when it came to Holly, though. 'I'll give you both a lift home,' came the deep voice of the man she'd been waiting to see all morning.

How long had he been standing there? Not

long or she'd have noticed. Her skin would've tingled, and her stomach tightened.

Got it bad, girl.

'Hi, Noah. You've heard the good news, then?'

Holly was staring him with a little smile. Oh, hell, now what?

Holly, meet your dad. Holly—

Stacey froze, staring at her girl, whose world was about to change radically. Not that Holly would understand much past 'This is Daddy'. If she understood that. Neither could she bring up the subject in front of the paediatrician and her entourage of nurses and registrar.

'You're okay with that? Last night you were happy for her to stay in as long as possible.'

'I hadn't expected her to improve so much. She's restless and being at home might be better for her, or for everyone else around here anyway.' Rubbing Holly's arm softly, she grinned. 'My girl's got some of her noise back.'

The paediatrician spoke to Noah. 'I'm very happy with the concussion, and Stacey's fully aware of what to look out for. As she says, little children do better at home surrounded by those who love them than in here, with strangers coming and going all the time.'

'I guess.' Noah sounded doubtful. The father in him coming out? Not the doctor?

Stacey laughed for the first time in days. 'She'll be fine, promise.'

'Mummy, I want a story.'

'What's the magic word?'

'Please.'

'Noah, can you stay with Holly while I get a book?' Deep breath. 'Holly, this is Noah, Mummy's friend.' Talk about a cliché.

Noah stepped forward. 'Hello, Holly. I see you banged your head.'

She raised her arm in front of him and knocked on the cast. 'It's broken.'

'That's not your head, silly billy.' Stacey tickled her under the chin. A giggle erupted from her girl, and Stacey relaxed some more. 'That's a very normal sound.'

Holly rubbed her forehead. 'Hurts, Mummy.'

'That's because you banged it. You've got to be careful.' She turned to Noah. 'Thanks for the offer of a lift but you don't have a car seat suitable for Holly.'

He pulled out his phone and brought up a picture of a car seat. 'There's this one or…' he flicked the screen '…this one. Both seem suitable but you need to make sure for me.'

She took the phone and studied the top-of-the-range seats. 'Either one will be ideal.'

'Good. I'll order it now and pick it up shortly.

I'd like to meet your parents again now that this is out in the open.'

'No problem. They want to talk to you, too.' She didn't like his controlled tone. Now he'd had more time to think about everything, had he come up with things not to his satisfaction?

'Do they? Good.' He sounded as though he expected them to give him a set of rules to follow, and that he already had his own ground rules to put in place.

'They want to clear the air and start over as they mean to go on.' She'd never seen him in this mood before and should've expected it. He'd had hours to go through everything, would've been churning things over and over. Now she needed to brace herself for the battle, for more questions fuelled by his doubts.

'Tell me about your previous relationship.'

Hadn't she already done that? *Stay calm.* They were in a ward with staff, patients and parents. This was not going to be the entertainment. Reaching the bed, she sat beside Holly and opened a book.

'Har-ree.' Holly pointed at the picture of the hairy monster.

'Sure is, sweetheart.' She began reading, ignoring Noah pacing over the small space between her and the window. Once the story was finished she handed over the book to Holly to run her fingers over the pictures. It would take a few minutes, giving her time to deal with Noah's question.

'Angus and I grew up two houses apart. We were playmates, then teenage friends, then we fell in love and finally got engaged. Then he met someone else.'

'How did you feel about that?'

'I was gutted. I loved him. I believed we were meant for each other.'

'And now?'

Her chest rose and fell. 'I'm over him. In a way he was right when he said we'd been friends too long before we became lovers and there was something missing from our relationship. It took me a while to see that.' It had taken Noah, and even then she wasn't trusting herself to believe she'd fallen for a man she'd only known for a few hours. 'Why's this important?'

His guard didn't slip. 'I know very little about you.'

About the mother of his child. She got it. He wasn't interested in her as a woman, and she'd best keep that in the forefront of her mind. Pain knocked her. So much for thinking they might have a future together. It wasn't happening. She had to be realistic. Rubbing her chest, she snapped, 'I could say the same about you, but I trust you to be considerate to me and Holly throughout what lies ahead,' and was pleased to see him jerk his head back.

'I've landed you with a child and no lead-in time.' At least she wasn't expecting marriage and a full-time relationship. Her heart ached for what could've been if only he felt the same. But she obviously hadn't done any more than turn him on for as long as it took to make love. Often. Watching Noah, the same tingling was going on in her palms, a familiar heat unfurling deep down, a longing she'd only known for him.

'So it would seem,' he said.

'You're still having doubts about Holly's paternity?' she demanded. 'We can have a DNA test done.' Her heart throbbed painfully at the thought of not still being believed over something so crucial.

Again Noah jerked his head and stared at her, his teeth digging into his bottom lip. After a long, leaden moment he shook his head. 'That won't be necessary, but thank you for understanding and offering.'

She didn't feel any relief. If anything, she was more uncomfortable. He was right about one thing. They didn't know each other, were mostly going on gut instinct. Which sometimes was safer than knowledge. Less overthinking.

'No, story.' Holly was holding out the book

Stacey had just read, this time towards Noah. 'No?'

'Noah, his name's Noah.' Or Daddy. Stacey gulped as she glanced at him. And was struck by the awe shining from him at his daughter. She could relax on Holly's behalf. This was going to work out for her, one way or another. But for *her*, she'd be waiting in the wings for any snippet of acknowledgement. No kisses, or passionate lovemaking. He wasn't interested in her.

Except there'd be a child's car seat ready by the end of the day so he could give them a lift. He had a way about him that brooked no argument when he was adamant about getting something. Another thing to watch out for when it came to discussing parenting with him.

At ten past five he appeared on the paediatric ward. 'Ready to go home?' he asked. 'I've got everything sorted.'

'She's been given the all clear as long as I stay at home with her tomorrow. I'd already arranged to take the day off. We'll see where we go after that. Dad's already put his hand up if I have to come in. There is a shortage of nurses due to the flu.'

'It's the same in Theatre,' Noah acknowledged. Then he turned to her and gave one of his heart-wrenching smiles. 'How're you feeling?'

Surprised. 'Happier now we're leaving here.' Deep breath.

Tell him what you think.

'Thanks for this. I'm glad you haven't walked away.'

Now who looked surprised? 'Anastasia…' Noah hesitated. Started again. 'I meant it when I said I won't do that. As you can imagine, I was awake most of the night, going over what you've told me, and I completely accept it's the truth.'

'Just like that?'

'Not quite. After my previous relationship I'm a little short on trust, but every argument I put up during the night crumbled away when I went through the little I know about you.'

Did that mean what it sounded like?

'I don't know where you and I are headed. I do know that from the moment we bumped into each other last Monday I've wanted to spend more time with you.'

Hope flared. She deliberately squashed it. 'Isn't it a bit soon to be telling me this? Shouldn't you wait until you've totally accepted your daughter into your life?'

Stepping closer, he continued. 'Maybe but when I think of Holly I always end up thinking about you instead. And, yes, I do question what you expect of me, and what you'll give back in return.'

Which was why he wanted more time. The hope disappeared. She couldn't blame him for that. It was a big ask to be accepted so easily. 'Guess you'll have to wait and see.' She lifted her girl into her arms. 'But first...' Deep breath. 'Holly, this is Daddy. Say, "Hello, Daddy."'

Holly grinned and stared at him. 'Hello, No.'

Noah laughed, not appearing at all disappointed. 'Does this mean "No" is going to be your favourite word, my girl, instead of yes? If so, we're in for some arguments.'

'No. No.' Holly banged her hand on Stacey's arms, and grinned some more.

The Wainwright house was a three-storey, semi-detached in neat condition with a tidy front lawn. Despite Holly having been in hospital, the gate onto the road was firmly shut. Noah shuddered at the thought of her running out and being hit by the kid on a skateboard. Turning back to his vehicle, he opened the rear door, unclipped Holly from her seat and handed her to Stacey. 'I'll grab the bag.'

Stacey handed Holly back. 'You carry her. I'll get that.'

His heart softened as he reached for his daughter. It was hard to get enough of her now he'd accepted parenthood. 'Thanks.' He leaned over and kissed Stacey's cheek, tried to ignore the jolt of longing that caught him. Backing off, he waited to follow her to the house.

She'd looked stunned then pleased at the kiss. Damn, he should've kept his emotions to himself. Now she'd be thinking he was ready for more with her. Not that he wouldn't enjoy making love again. His body was wired for hers, rarely quietened when around her. But to take Anastasia to bed now would be wrong, and unkind. It would suggest nothing had changed, that they were still seeing each other as two people without a child between them, and before both of them had worked out what they wanted for the future. He was presuming Stacey hadn't too many expectations of him and her position in his life.

The front door opened before they reached the steps. 'Holly, sweetheart, you're home. She's looking better, Stacey.' Ian Wainwright stood there, looking relaxed and pleased to see them all. Even him. 'Hello, Noah.'

Noah stuck his hand out. 'Ian, I hope I'm not inconveniencing you.'

'Of course not. You're welcome to visit anytime.' He wasn't saying who he should be visiting. Holly or Stacey? 'Come in out of the cold.' His welcome was genuine, like his daughter.

It was like stepping into the past. Laughter came from another room, music was playing in the background, the smell of dinner cooking reached his nostrils and warmed him. Noah closed his eyes and breathed deeply, drew up memories of when he'd been a little boy. 'Wonderful.'

'It is, isn't it?' Caution laced Stacey's question.

'You're lucky.'

'I know, though sometimes I take it all for granted.'

Judy appeared in the kitchen doorway and crossed to lift her granddaughter out of his arms. 'Hello, sweetheart. Grandma's happy to see you.' Kiss, kiss, kiss on Holly's cheeks. Then she smiled at Noah. 'You'll stay for dinner.'

Did he have a choice? He chuckled. 'I'd love to.'

'I'll heat up some baked beans for Holly and you can sit with her while she eats.' Stacey grinned. Which was the first easy grin he'd had from her in days.

It warmed his heart and relaxed some of the tension that had built up on the short drive from the hospital. 'Is my shirt going to survive?'

Stacey's spread hand flipped back and forth. 'Maybe.'

Only one red splotch marred the front of his white shirt by the time Holly decided she'd had enough and shoved the plate aside. 'Read me a story, No.'

'What's the magic word?' her mother asked from the kitchen, where she was helping her mother.

'Please, No.'

'Please, Daddy.' Stacey had come to stand in the doorway. 'Noah is your daddy.'

'No Daddy?' Those beautiful eyes were huge in the tiny face.

'Yes, Daddy,' he growled around a blockage in his throat.

'No, Daddy.' The little minx giggled.

Reaching for her, Noah wrapped his daughter in his arms and kissed the top of her head. His heart was pounding, his throat still blocked, and when he glanced across to Stacey she was wiping her eyes with the back of her hand. Anastasia was full of love for so many people. She was happy for him to be a part of Holly's life, had offered to have a DNA test for his peace of mind.

In his arms, Holly began wriggling to get down. 'Careful or you'll hurt your arm,' he cautioned in a croaky voice. Setting her carefully on her feet, he watched her dash across to Granddad and scramble up onto his knees.

'It's bedtime, missy,' Ian said as he hugged her.
'No.'

No as in Noah, or, no, I don't want to go to bed?

Noah grinned. This was family, right here in this old-fashioned sweet house that was so different from the modern sterile place he lived in. This was what he remembered from his childhood—not the house and its fixtures but the genuine love and kindness, the acceptance of each other. It was perfect. Happiness crept under his ribs. Unbelievable. Everything he wanted was right here. If he dared take a chance.

Another glance at Stacey had his heart dancing again, this time for her. And them. Could it be as easy as saying, 'Come with me and make magic, bring up our daughter together and be happy?' Could he trust himself to make that decision?

'Stacey, it's Noah. You wanted me?' Wednesday and she was back at work. They might get to steal a few minutes together throughout the day. According to the nurses, she'd been trying to get hold of him for the last hour while he'd been in surgery.

'Jonathon Black's got another problem, more pain in the abdomen. It's severe. The registrar's seen him and thinks you should take a look.'

'Can you put him on?' He'd get the details

and suggest what would be necessary until he finished in Theatre.

Then he recalled what she'd said the first time she'd phoned him to see Jonathon. She'd rightly suspected appendicitis. 'Forget it. I'm on my way.' He was going to be unpopular either way he did this, and if Black was seriously ill again then that was more important than delaying an operation.

The lift doors swished open, reminding him what he should be focused on. Heading directly to the room where Jonathon had spent the last couple of weeks, he hesitated at the door when he saw Stacey talking to his patient. His heart did a little dance. No hesitation there. It was his mind that kept throwing up reasons not to get too involved. And frankly he was over what his mind was trying to do to his hopes.

He hadn't been cautious the first time round, but he was being so this time, and it was getting uncomfortable. If he wasn't careful, Stacey and Holly would bear the brunt of his past. As if Stacey would deliberately hurt him. What he saw and knew would be what he got and more, and that was good—kind, loving and fun. Heart and mind were getting mixed up now. Time to take a break.

But it wasn't that simple. The Wainwrights were friendly and caring, open and sharing.

Which was Stacey through and through. That's what he remembered and had longed for since that fatal night when Robert had come to tell him his parents had died. After his blunder with Christine he'd thought he'd never find it. Now he might have it with Anastasia. Might, but he was not totally convinced his heart was right.

There was no denying his attraction for her physically. It was strong and kept him awake most nights. So why not find out if he could live without Stacey in his life? There was doubt there already: it just needed looking into further. There was only one way to find out and that was by shoving caution aside to spend more time with her, starting with asking her out for a meal one night this week.

Decision made, he walked over to his patient. 'I hear you're in pain again, Jonathon. Whereabouts?'

Stacey helped Jonathon lift the sheet and pull his hospital gown up to expose his belly.

'All around here.' With his palm, Jonathon touched most of his abdomen. 'It's not like the last twice. It's more a widespread ache, worse when I cough or go to the bathroom.'

'Any nausea?' Noah gently probed the abdomen.

'Every time I eat or drink. And the pain gets worse about half an hour after eating.'

'Can I see the notes?' he asked Stacey, and took the proffered board.

Flicking through Jonathon's history, he could find nothing to raise alarm bells. But the blood tests showed not everything was settling down as quickly from the appendicitis as he'd hoped. An underlying cause? Another problem they hadn't known about?

'We need more blood tests done. When did you last eat?'

'Breakfast.'

'Four hours ago,' Stacey informed him.

'The pain was excruciating then.'

Diverticulitis? 'Right, no more food by mouth. Stacey'll set you up with intravenous nutrition via fluids. I'm prescribing stronger antibiotics and arranging a CT scan of your bowel.' Turning to Stacey, he added, 'Liver functions, urine and stool samples, please.'

When they were well away from Jonathon's room, Stacey asked, 'What are you thinking?'

'Diverticulitis.'

'Another severe infection. What's going on?' She was on to it straight away.

'I'm going to arrange further screening to see if there's an underlying cause that we haven't found yet. The cancer could be in other organs, though symptoms haven't presented.' Though that didn't feel right.

Stacey's face fell. 'He doesn't deserve that. He's so sweet and nice to everyone, even when we're doing awful procedures on him.'

No one deserved cancer, but he agreed with her. 'Fingers crossed I'm wrong. Let me know as soon as you get the lab results.' He turned for the lift, paused, and returned to Stacey, his heart hammering. She might think he wanted to soften any blow he might have for the future. But he hadn't decided completely on what he had to offer yet, was afraid of getting it wrong and losing any chance of working this out so that all three of them were happy. 'I thought we might go out for dinner on Friday night if that suits you.'

'I usually spend the nights with Holly. If you'd like—'

The emergency buzzer screamed throughout the ward.

Stacey leapt around the counter to read the number flashing from the screen. 'Bed eleven. Cardiac arrest. Jason, resus cart.' And she was gone, Jason right beside her with the cart.

Noah was on her heels. 'Who is it?'

'Fifty-five-year-old female, post gastro surgery, history of cardiac arrest, last time six months ago.' She raced into the room. 'Keep doing compressions, Ada. Jason, prepare the defib.' She tore the woman's gown open and pressed the patches onto the woman's skin before attaching the leads and reading the monitor.

Noah took the electric pads from Jason. The screen showed the heart had stopped. 'Stand back.'

Everyone else put space between themselves and the bed.

Stacey watched the screen.

Noah tapped the button on the defib.

Melissa's body jerked upwards.

Stacey watched the line on the screen, said calmly, 'Prepare for another shock.'

Noah primed the defibrillator. 'Stand back.'

The flat line rose and fell, trailing a pattern matching life. Then it stopped.

'Prepare for another shock,' Stacey ordered.

Shock. Jerk. The line rose, fell, rose, fell.

Noah was holding his breath, and when he looked around he saw everyone was doing the same. Except Stacey. She had a stethoscope to her ears and was listening to the woman's chest. Not satisfied with the monitor? Not taking anything for granted? That was Stacey. Finally she straightened. 'Well done, everyone. Jason, stay with Melissa. She's your sole charge for the rest of the day. I'll phone her surgeon and let him know what's happened, though I doubt he's going to be surprised.' Then she turned to him. 'Noah, do you think you could examine our patient so I can report back to her surgeon?'

'Of course. Where are her notes?'

'Here.' Jason extended a file.

After a quick appraisal of the woman's history of heart surgeries and the recent gastro op, her temperature, heart rate before and after the arrest, her blood flow before checking the wound for sepsis, Noah said, 'All clean. She hasn't complained of pain any time today?'

Ada shook her head. 'No. In fact, she was saying she hadn't felt so good for months.'

Hadn't he heard that often enough to almost take it as a warning something was about to happen? After a thorough examination, he told Stacey and Jason, 'I can't find anything that might've triggered that attack other than her history of cardiac failures. But her surgeon should see her ASAP.'

'He's on his way,' Stacey informed him.

'Then I'll get back to Theatre.' He'd nearly reached the lift when he heard Stacey call out.

'Noah.' She approached with what he thought was apprehension. 'About Friday night? We're spending time together seeing your relatives on Saturday. Can we leave it at that for now?'

'If that's what you want.' Disappointment at

not having time alone with her touched him. But, then, he didn't want to rush anything, did he?

'I'll bring Holly, too.'

That would cause a stir with the relatives for sure. But they had to find out sooner or later as he didn't intend hiding his daughter from anyone. 'Good idea.'

Relief poured into her face. 'Glad you think so.' She gave him such a sad smile he found himself wanting to banish it by saying they'd get through this okay and to haul her into his arms, hug her hard, but the lift doors opened behind him and Melissa's surgeon, Connor Harrison, charged out.

'Stacey, is Melissa conscious?'

'Yes,' she answered, still looking at him. 'Noah checked Melissa over.'

'Noah, thanks for that. Talk later. I need to see her.' Connor headed down the ward.

'I'd better join him,' Stacey said, but she didn't move.

'I'd better get on with surgery. Talk to you later about Saturday.'

'Looking forward to it.' She gave him a wave over her shoulder as she chased after Connor.

She wouldn't be looking forward to meeting Robert and Alice if she knew how cold they were. Not even Stacey's friendly disposition would warm their hearts. Noah watched until she disappeared into Melissa's room. She certainly did things to his heart that he wasn't used to. Was this what he'd been looking for? The feeling of coming home when he'd walked into her parents' house yesterday said so. How did he know for certain? By taking time to find out more, and waiting to see if he did love her, or if this was a passing fancy.

Time to get back to work. Phoning downstairs, he told them he was on his way.

CHAPTER NINE

STACEY'S STOMACH WAS tied in knots when Noah arrived to pick them up on Saturday. They weren't going to stay long at his relatives' house as Holly might get grumpy, as she did sometimes when she couldn't do something because of the cast, and Noah said it wouldn't work to put her down for a nap there. He wouldn't explain why, just said that afterwards they'd go to his place for a while so he'd have more time with Holly.

As he opened the back door to his four-wheel drive, he leaned in and kissed Holly on the cheek. 'Hello, Holly.'

'Hello, No Daddy.'

Stacey's heart wobbled. At least these two were getting along. If only she and Noah could make headway. They got on fine at work, where nothing personal came up, but away from the hospital there was an undercurrent of uncertainty running between them that had started when she'd told him he was Holly's father, and so far nothing had seemed to change it.

Then he surprised her with a kiss on her cheek. Chaste and still making her heart beat harder than normal. 'Noah?'

He breathed deeply. 'Citrus. That tangy, sweet smell always reminds me of you.'

'Are you trying to butter me up?' she asked, a little too abruptly.

'Not at all. Just stating a fact.' His smile was skewwhiff.

Trying for relaxed, she smiled. 'Lemons and oranges, my lasting impression, huh?'

'One of them.'

She wasn't asking what the others were. She had enough of her own about Noah to make her blush if he knew what she was thinking. She handed Holly over to him to put in the car seat. 'I've brought a colouring-in book and pencils to keep her occupied at the house. Do I need to grab some paper to protect any surfaces?'

Noah shook his head. 'I'm sure Jackson will rustle up something.'

'Who's Jackson?'

'The butler.'

Her stomach dropped. The butler. Just where were they going? Here she'd been worrying if Noah's aunt and uncle would accept her and Holly, and now there was a butler in the picture. That spoke volumes, told her she had no idea what the morning would bring. She wasn't against butlers as such, but a sense of being out of her depth was creeping in and they hadn't left Harlow yet.

She climbed into the vehicle, laid the flowers she'd bought on the floor by her feet, and strapped herself in tight, then looked at her outfit. Black leggings under a short red skirt, a fitted floral blouse and a tight corduroy jacket. She'd splashed out in the winter sales for those items, and then had really blown the budget with new—no nicks and scratches—black, knee-high boots, so she was dressed up for the occasion, and now she felt cheap.

Noah wore navy trousers and jacket, offset with a cream shirt and blue tie. Classy without going over the top. Not that she knew a lot about classy, but he looked good enough to eat. Now, there was a thought.

The back door closed, then the vehicle rocked as Noah got into the driver's seat. 'Ready?'

As she'd ever be, which was never. 'Yes.' Then, 'Why are you taking me to meet your relatives when you don't seem to like them much?'

Good point. Noah still couldn't get his head around the fact he'd invited Anastasia to Robert and Alice's. It was a step forward, introducing her to his family in case they got together permanently. And also to finally lay his doubts to rest when Stacey saw the property. She'd be amazed, and stoic, and get on with being polite and keeping Holly amused. Not like his aunt. Alice had been her usual frosty self when he'd said he was bringing a friend and her daughter to meet them.

'I hope she's got class, Noah.'

Oh, Anastasia was classy all right, just not aloof and a boorish snob. 'She's a wonderful woman.' Anastasia was no mug, and certainly could hold her own, but so could Alice. He didn't want Anastasia feeling hurt or upset over anything that might be said today. He shouldn't be taking her there. He straightened his back. He'd support her, no matter what, show Robert and Alice who was important in his life.

'Are flowers all right for your aunt?' Anastasia asked tightly.

'Of course they are. You didn't have to do that.' Though Alice would be miffed if she hadn't.

'I think I do.' Her smile was brief.

Fingers crossed for a smile of any sort during the next couple of hours. 'I hope you're comfortable with this visit,' he reiterated.

'Noah, hush. You've already warned me it might be a little cool, and I'm prepared. I can be well mannered if required. Which usually means saying very little.' Her attempt at laughing at herself fell flat when she started staring out the window.

'I'm going to tell them Holly's my daughter.'

Her head spun round. 'You're sure about that?'

'Absolutely.' Introducing Holly into the mix would raise more questions, but he was prepared for those. She was his daughter, and that, Robert and Alice, was that.

'Good.' Her fingers on her free hand were clenched, not exactly backing up that comment. Then she added, 'Thanks. It means a lot that you're accepting Holly completely.'

Time for some light relief. 'Did you bring some music for our girl to break the boredom of travelling?'

Relief filled her face. 'Sure did.'

Soon the sound of squeaky voices that kids apparently liked filled the interior and Holly was joining in. Noah began to relax.

Finally when he pulled through the gate and started up the long sweeping drive lined with old oak trees, his breath caught in the back of his throat and he was afraid to look at his companion in case he saw an expression that would tell him he'd got it all wrong, that she did want a lifestyle unknown to her and attainable only by fooling him.

Anastasia said nothing until he pulled up outside the wide stairs leading to the front door and she turned to him. 'What a beautiful home.' There was nothing but genuine honesty in her face. No avarice or hope or envy.

Noah exhaled. 'You're right. It is.'

'Has it always been in your family?'

'About two hundred and twenty years. Robert was the oldest brother so it was passed down to him, and my cousin is next in line to own it.' He was still looking for a reaction that would scream a warning. When none came, he expanded. 'Thank goodness. I don't want to live here. It was bad enough in the times I had to come back during holidays. Large, cold rooms that go on for ever. No small, comfortable spaces to be happy in.'

'Oh, Noah.' Her hand enveloped his, squeezed tight. 'That's hideous.'

One word for it. 'Yes. Shall we go in?' Of course neither Alice nor Robert had come to the door to greet them, but Jackson was waiting. Thank goodness some delightful things never changed. Out of the car, he went to get Holly but Anastasia had beaten him to it, clinging to her like a shield.

She looked around once and then at him, her shoulders suddenly tense. 'Do I look all right?'

Wrapping an arm around her, he tucked her in against him and shut the car door. 'You're beautiful.' He wasn't lying. Her gleaming dark blonde hair spilled down her back and her funky red earrings bobbed whenever she turned her head. 'You're not on display.' But Alice would take note of every piece of clothing and the hairstyle and those earrings. Damn the woman. Not everyone lived like her, and she'd never accepted that because it was her right to lord it over people about how she was married to a Kennedy.

Tempting as it was to drive away for a relaxed lunch somewhere else, it couldn't happen. He'd told Robert he'd come, and that meant he had to. And sometime soon he had to let his relatives know he was a father anyway. May as well get that over with.

Taking a quick look around at the familiar land sprawled out beyond the mansion, he thought about those relaxed years in Auckland that already seemed a lifetime ago. Stacey had hit the nail on the head when she'd asked why he'd left there when he was happy. If only he could've stayed on down under and ignored the family for good. But irresponsibility wasn't one of his flaws.

He'd never intended to stay away quite as long as he had, but the months had got away from him as he'd worked with some amazing and friendly plastic surgeons, constantly perfecting his skill level. In reality, he had missed London and his friends, and the gnawing need to find Anastasia just to put his mind at rest that she wasn't the right one for him had also played a part in buying a ticket home.

He breathed deeply. His mouth dried. His gut churned. Goosebumps rose on his arms. Citrus. Anastasia's scent. Her mark on him. A scent he couldn't forget, or their time together that one night. Drawing in another huge lungful of air, the tang of lemons and oranges teased his senses, and set his blood humming. No getting away from that smell that had haunted him for so long. 'Come on. Let's get inside where hopefully there's a fire roaring in some room.'

Stacey shivered, and not from the cold. She shouldn't have come. The house was formidable. From another world, and made her feel inferior, which she shouldn't. She was no different from Noah. Their emotions were the same, they ate meals and worked in a hospital, they were parents to Holly. She shivered again. And he was wealthy beyond her comprehension. This was a timely wake-up call. They couldn't be together. She didn't belong. The night she'd gone to his house in the city she hadn't taken a lot of notice, having been too interested in Noah himself, and where their kisses had been leading. This place was intimidating and she hadn't gone inside yet. Though that was only a few steps from becoming real.

'Good morning, Noah.' The older man in a black suit standing erect at the door smiled happily. 'It's good to see you.'

'Jackson, great to see you, too.' Noah hugged him. 'How have you been?'

'Can't complain. Nobody listens.' The man laughed.

'Jackson, this is Anastasia Wainwright, a friend and colleague of mine. And our daughter, Holly.'

Stacey gasped. Noah had told the butler Holly was his daughter? Just like that? Wow. She could love him for that alone. And the fact he obviously treated everyone with respect and genuine friendliness. Some of her concerns backed off. He would always be caring for her and Holly. How was she going to sort this conundrum out? She loved Noah but did she love him enough to accept all that came with him? When he stood up for her by speaking out about Holly then, yes, she could. She held her hand out to shake Jackson's. 'Glad to meet you,' she said with a smile.

'You, too, Anastasia. I hope this young man is looking after you.'

Putting a finger to her lips, she pondered the question, and finally said, 'Can't say I have any complaints.'

'Phew. I was waiting with bated breath.' Noah smiled as though he'd truly been worried. Maybe he had, though not likely about any complaints she might come up with, but more along the lines of regretting bringing her here.

'Let's go inside.' Noah took her elbow.

'Your aunt and uncle are in the conservatory,' Jackson informed Noah as he closed the door after them.

Stacey felt Noah flinch. He wasn't happy about which room they were going to?

'Thank you, Jackson.' Then to Stacey he said with an annoyed smile, 'It's all right. The conservatory will be very warm.'

But the occupants mightn't be? Was that the cause of that tight expression? She leaned closer briefly. 'Everything's fine.'

'Yes, of course.'

She'd never heard Noah speak so sharply. She didn't feel this was about her and Holly, but more about his family. Talking to Jackson, he'd relaxed a little, but that had changed in an instant. Interesting, and worrying. She didn't want Noah unhappy. It didn't bode well for the coming hour.

Noah strode into the conservatory. With his hand still on her elbow, Stacey struggled to keep up with him, so her entrance was less than gracious. Gracious? What sort of word was that in her life? A quick glance around at the perfectly potted plants and polished leather chairs and she instantly felt out of place. Then her eyes spied two people sitting very straight in large, uncomfortable-looking seats, watching her and Noah, and Holly. Yes, the woman's eyes widened as they landed on Holly.

'Robert, Aunt Alice.' Noah bobbed his head. His mouth lifted into a facsimile of a smile, nothing like the ones he usually gave her that turned her to mush.

She moved as close to him as possible without looking like she was his pet.

Robert stood up, crossed to give Noah a perfunctory slap on the back. 'Glad you could come.'

Noah nodded. 'This is Anastasia Wainwright, a friend of mine. Stacey, my Aunt Alice and Uncle Robert.'

Stacey stepped forward, holding her hand out. 'Pleased to meet you, Robert.'

The handshake was short and sharp. 'And I you, Anastasia.'

She stepped around him and approached Noah's aunt, who was appraising her. And coming up with not a lot for recommendation if that blank expression meant anything. 'I'm Stacey and I work in the same hospital as Noah. These are for you.' She presented the bouquet of flowers she'd been gripping while holding Holly. They looked battered and bruised.

'You're a doctor?' Surprise brought some animation to the woman's face as she took the proffered flowers and immediately handed them to Jackson.

'Not at all. I'm a nurse and love it.'

'A very good one, too,' Noah added from directly behind her.

She hadn't heard him move, or sensed his proximity, which showed how this woman was unnerving her.

Well, I might not be rich or have the dress sense of the famous, but I am genuine and love my family and life.

'Thank you.' She smiled at Noah.

Noah straightened his already straight back. 'And this is our daughter, Holly.'

'Right.' Robert stepped nearer. 'Take a seat. Jackson, would you please bring Noah and Anastasia something to drink.' He totally ignored Holly.

Stacey glanced at Alice, saw incredulity on her face. Why? Noah was capable of fathering a child. Even with her. No wonder he wasn't overly happy with these people. They were cold, and aloof. What had that done to a grieving ten-year-old boy needing someone to love him? She sank onto the nearest chair, cuddling Holly closer. Holly seemed to sense the atmosphere because she was unusually quiet, too.

'A glass of wine, Anastasia?' Jackson asked with a friendly smile.

Was Jackson his first or last name? She hoped it was his first name. Calling someone by their surname didn't sit comfortably. 'Yes, please, Jackson. A pinot noir, if that's possible?' A very large one, please.

'Of course. What would Holly like? An orange juice, perhaps?'

'She'd love that.'

'No problem.' He was still smiling when he turned to Noah. 'A chardonnay for you?'

'A very small one, thanks.' Noah sat in the chair next to her. 'Where are the others?' he asked Robert.

'Unfortunately your cousins have had to cancel,' Robert answered. 'Perhaps you and I could go to my study before Jackson brings the wine.

There are a couple of issues I need to discuss with you.'

'Good idea.'

Stacey saw Noah's slight shrug as he stood up again. Who was this Noah? No one she'd met before. There wasn't any love going round as there would be at her home. Not that her family made an issue of it. It was just there in the way they spoke to each other.

'I won't be long, Anastasia. If Holly gets restless, sit her at that low table where she can colour her pictures.'

'Will do.' And she'd try to ignore that glare from Alice.

'Mummy, down.'

Great. 'Shall we do some colouring in?'

'What happened to her arm?' Alice asked.

'She was knocked over by a kid on a skateboard.'

'Should she be on the road at her age?'

'Someone left the gate open.' Placing pencils and the colouring book in front of Holly, Stacey sat back on her ankles and looked around the room. 'You've got some wonderful paintings in here.'

'Yes, I'm a bit of a collector. Do you like art yourself?'

'I know very little about it. Just like what I like without understanding the nuances.'

'At least you're honest.' For a moment Alice seemed to relax with her. She stared at a painting in front of her. 'I used to dabble in art myself, but unfortunately I wasn't very good.'

'That's a shame.'

'Oh, well, can't be helped. Ah, here are our drinks.'

Stacey almost felt sorry for this woman, stuck in this massive house and not doing the things she got enjoyment from. Though she seemed to enjoy being the hostess, even to Stacey, someone they clearly wouldn't have expected Noah to bring home.

Then Noah was back, and she could relax more. Concentrating on keeping Holly happy, she let most of the conversation go over her head, until Noah stood up. 'Right, we'd better be heading back to the city before Holly gets too tired. She's recovering from an accident and needs special attention at the moment.'

Then Stacey got a shock as she lifted Holly into her arms.

Alice came across and lightly ran a finger down Holly's cheek. 'Thank you for visiting us, Holly.' It was the first real acknowledgement there'd been that Holly even existed.

Stacey looked at Noah, and saw him swallowing hard, shock registering on his face. She hugged her daughter. She'd done what no one else seemed to have. She'd got through to Alice.

Noah gulped. Alice had gone to Holly and touched her cheek. Like she cared for his daughter. Hell, she'd never once been so kind to him. Not even when his heart had been broken and he'd been missing his parents desperately.

He stared at this stranger. Alice? Seriously? He didn't know whether to laugh or cry. The young boy who'd wanted only to be loved had not known this woman to have a gentle side.

And now she was talking to Holly.

And Holly was smiling back, as she always did, believing everyone was as kind and loving as her mother's family.

Noah shook his head. Unbelievable. But it didn't alter a thing when it came to sorting out the future. That belonged entirely to Anastasia and himself.

On Monday Stacey was getting up to speed with patients that had been admitted over the weekend when Noah showed up on the ward.

'How was the rest of your weekend?' he asked, without checking if anyone was within hearing.

'Quiet. Holly still gets tired quickly.'

'Can the three of us spend some time together at my house next weekend?' He looked tired too.

Guess this was part of settling everything into place. 'Sure. I'd like that,' she added, because it was true. She'd spent most of yesterday thinking about Noah and his relatives and just what he might want to do about their future.

'You're being generous with your time and daughter.' He smiled.

Which stirred her from head to toe. 'Only way to go,' she said truthfully. No point in worrying if she was doing the wrong thing. Holly deserved her father in her life, and this way her mother would be there too, assessing everything for the time a decision had to be made.

Damn it, she couldn't be blushing. But something was turning her skin red hot. Thank goodness no other staff were at their desks. 'We do seem to connect, don't we?'

'Very well.' Another smile to tighten her stomach. 'I'd better get a wriggle on with seeing my patients. The surgical list is long today.'

Stacey picked up the pile of files she'd already prepared and followed him in to see Jonathon, who was getting fed up with being stuck in hospital and showing it.

'The infection in your bowel has lessened off enough that you should be able to go home on Wednesday,' Noah told him. Turning to Stacey, he added, 'I'll fill out a lab form for more blood tests before I head downstairs.'

On the way to the next patient, he said quietly, 'See you for breakfast one morning? I'm on call all week so won't get away at other times easily.'

'I'll be in the cafeteria every morning,' she said with a grin.

'I'm discharging Ben Ibbotson today. He needs to have weekly physio appointments and a follow-up with me in two weeks,' Noah told her.

'All sorted,' Stacey replied.

'Good. Now, Linda Garrick.' He turned into the opposite room. 'Morning, Linda. How're you today?'

'Fine, Doctor. I've been walking up and down the ward for thirty minutes and while the wound is painful I got along quite well.'

'Very well, from what I saw,' Stacey added.

'Don't get too carried away,' Noah told his patient. 'After such a deep tear, that calf muscle is going to take time to fully heal.'

It was a typical ward round, and afterwards Noah stayed a few minutes, talking about his patients, dropping in a few smiles for her when he thought no one was looking.

Though Liz seemed to notice everything. 'You sure you haven't got something going with our hot surgeon?' she asked as Stacey tried not to watch Noah striding along to the lift, his shoulders back and his head high.

Stacey wasn't sure about anything except she was falling deeper in love with Noah, and still didn't know where they were headed. 'It's great catching up with him again.'

Liz snorted. 'I might not be the brightest lightbulb in the room but I ain't blind.'

She laughed. What else could she do? If she said anything Liz would put her own interpretation on it and probably be closer to the truth than Stacey wanted anyone to get.

They managed two shared breakfasts over the week, her parents enthusiastically pushing her out the door with promises of getting Holly up and fed before taking her to the nursery or settling down for the day at home with Granddad. Stacey skipped onto the train and off at the other end, racing to the hospital cafeteria for toast and coffee, and time with Noah, deliberately forgetting the issues between them. It was great just to have time alone with him. And in the evenings, after dinner was over, the dishes were stacked in the dishwasher, and she'd read the requisite stories to Holly, she'd phone Noah. 'How was your day, apart from a perforated lung and an appendectomy?'

'You missed out the three hernias.'

'They didn't come to our ward. Holly said goodnight to Daddy tonight.'

'She did? Cool.' Noah sighed. For the first time in days he sounded irritated.

'Something wrong?' she asked, apprehension tightening her throat.

'What do you want? How do you see this working out? Why haven't you said anything about this, Anastasia?'

Anastasia, but not the having-fun one. Pounding set up behind her ribs. This discussion had been lurking in the background even during the fun moments, no matter how hard she'd tried to deny it. 'I've been giving you time to come to terms with being a dad.'

'Right. I'm there. Tell me what you want.'

'It's hard. I've been Holly's mother all her short life, been there for her all the time other than when I've gone to work. I can't imagine any other way to raise my child.' She certainly didn't want to divide the time with her father.

'She has two parents now.'

'I know what that entails. I really do.' She could hardly say she wanted to be with him as his partner or wife. He'd gag on that.

There was a silence that seemed to get heavier by the second. Then, 'We'll talk over the weekend.'

'Okay.' She could let it go for now and enjoy

the relief of not coming to a final decision just yet. More time to enjoy as a solo parent.

Noah found a bottle of headache pills and swallowed two. His head had been pounding all morning. The week had been long and tedious. All he'd wanted was to spend time with Anastasia; to make love, to talk and laugh and share everything. Okay, he'd fallen for her fast. Too fast? Or had this been three years in the making and now he'd caught up with her he wanted to make up for lost time? That was more likely the answer, and the deeper in love he became, the more the warning bells tolled. What if he was wrong? Well, today he was about to find out, as Anastasia and Holly would be here soon.

Anastasia had been completely honest with him about Holly. She seemed to enjoy his company, giving him a sense that she had feelings for him beyond a friend who had a child with her. She didn't appear to be out for all she could get. She hadn't gone all simpering or gushing when he'd shown her around the house, hadn't made overtures about how Holly would be happy here and how she'd have to accompany her daughter if she was to spend time with him.

Yet the past kept waving at him, reminding him how easily he'd been duped before. But Anastasia didn't know coldness of the heart. It wasn't in her. What if they married? Would she make demands on him as his ex had? Would she always be wanting more and more, never satisfied with what she had? Given how she was happy with the little she did have, he couldn't see her changing radically. On the other hand, suddenly finding herself well off might be a catalyst to going overboard and needing to spend large and become fixated with the whole lifestyle he was desperate to avoid.

Ding-dong. The doorbell rang out.

His heart lifted. Anastasia and his daughter were here. *Their* daughter. He had to let go of the past if he wanted to find true happiness, something he suspected was on his doorstep right now if only he found the courage to follow his heart. He would be the one to lose out if he got this wrong. And the last thing he wanted to lose was Anastasia. She was his other half, if only she recognised that. She had to. He finally had. Deep breath. Yes, damn it. He did. He loved Stacey and Holly.

Pulling the door wide, he gazed at the two females who had his head in a spin. It wasn't hard to smile wide and deep. 'Hey, come in. I'm glad you're here.' He really was. All the doubts had taken a back seat the moment his gaze came to rest on Anastasia. Leaning in, he kissed her briefly.

Her return kiss was quieter than he'd become used to, and he'd have thought she'd changed her mind about being with him if he hadn't seen the flicker of need in her eyes. Closing the door, he led them down to the kitchen and the alcove on the side where he'd set out an array of toys he'd bought during the week.

Holly made a beeline for them and plopped down on her backside, reaching for the doll dressed in pink.

'That's a hit.' Anastasia smiled, the visible tightness in her shoulders loosening as she sat on a stool at the counter.

'Coffee?'

'You're a lifesaver. There wasn't any at home. Someone stuffed up the shopping yesterday.'

'Whose job is it usually?' From what he'd seen, the Wainwrights seemed to share all the chores around the house.

'Anyone who has an hour to spare. Which wasn't me, what with taking Holly to see the paediatrician after I finished my shift.'

'She got a good report.' Anastasia had filled him in last night. 'Hard to keep her down, isn't it?'

'Sure is. I hope you haven't got anything precious lying around at her level.' She scoped the room.

'I spent time putting things out of reach this morning.'

When Holly became bored with the toys, they took her into the sitting room with the piano and she created noise that only doting parents could cope with. After lunch they strolled along the streets and when Holly grizzled Noah piggy-backed her the rest of the way.

'She needs to have a sleep,' Anastasia said as they returned to the house.

'I've set up the room next to my office as a bedroom for now.' Breath held, he waited to see what her reaction would be.

'Lovely, thank you.'

She lifted Holly down from his back. 'Hey, darling, how was that?'

'Good. Daddy horse.'

He laughed. 'I've got my uses. I'll fetch your bag. I presume you need it to change Holly.'

'Thanks.' Anastasia was totally focused on her girl.

He felt almost redundant but then she was used to doing all this herself. Even when her parents were at home she did most of it, she'd told him. *I am her mum.*

It would be different if they were together, living under the same roof, sharing the responsibilities. He'd definitely do his share of whatever was required. Damn it, he wanted to be doing it now.

'Here.' He walked into Holly's room and handed Anastasia the bag, the questions churning in his head. He knew what he wanted, he didn't know if he could ask for it. 'How long will Holly sleep?'

'About two hours, if I'm lucky.'

We, not I. Noah kept that to himself. No point in aggravating her. There were more important things to say once they were out in the warm conservatory.

Within minutes Holly had fallen asleep and Anastasia led him out and closed the door quietly, leaving behind a monitor so she'd know if Holly cried.

'Would you like a glass of wine?' he asked.

'That'd be nice.' She still wasn't as relaxed with him as she'd been other times. Because Holly was here? Or something else?

When they were sitting, glasses in hand, he asked, 'What made you want to be a nurse?'

As they chatted about everyday subjects the tension left Anastasia and she became animated in the way he adored. Listening to her talking about her need to be the best in her nursing class, why she loved dancing so much, how her dad had taught her to be strong through his own traumas, reinforced why he loved her.

And then she asked, 'Are you settling back into London life?'

There'd been too many shocks for that. First the extent of Robert's debts and what Noah was expected to do about them, then learning he was a father. And especially his feelings for Anastasia. They had blown him out of the water. 'I've had too many other things on my mind to think about it.'

'I guess you have a lot on your plate.' Her hands were tightening.

'I've finalised everything with Robert and got him out of the jam he was in.' May as well let her know a little of his family's problems. 'He got into debt and needed me to save his butt. It's what our family does. Up to a point anyway. I've now locked things up legally so he can't go off the edge again.'

'Fair enough.'

'That was the main reason I came home, and once here I saw that if I didn't stay to keep an eye on things, Robert would only make other mistakes.'

'Then you bought into a private practice and took up the job at London Riverside.' There was a sharpness creeping into her voice.

What was that about? 'I *am* a surgeon. I'm not going to sit around not using my skills. What's this about, Stacey? You seem upset.'

She locked her eyes on him. 'I understand you're busy, and life as you saw it has changed drastically with the advent of Holly. How do you see her and I fitting in with you?'

He sat up straighter, his chin lifting. 'Actually, that's one problem I have put some thought into.'

'Problem? I see.' Anger flashed across her face, gone as quickly as it rose. 'I understand this has been a shock, but if we're being designated to the problem basket then please don't give it another thought. We'll be on our way home and out of your way for good.'

Damn. He'd gone and blown it. He needed to approach this slowly, carefully. 'Anastasia.' She winced. 'Stacey, I didn't mean it like that. You're not a problem. It's just that there are no simple answers. I'm getting comfortable with being a father and want to have a bigger part in Holly's life.'

She continued to watch him without saying a word. Waiting for what?

'And I want to be a part of your life. I would like to share raising Holly as a family, not take turns. I've longed for a family to love and cherish, and I could have that with you and Holly.' Deep breath. 'Would you marry me?' So much for slow and careful. But why procrastinate? He knew what he wanted. He'd admitted to himself he loved Anastasia, so there was no reason to hold back.

'Why should I do that?' Her words were sharp, like small pebbles slapping into mud.

'We connect whenever we're together.' Except right now. 'We could raise Holly together, living here so we both can be a part of her life every day.'

So I can see you, love you, share everything I've got with you.

'You could become a full-time mum if you want to.' Her expression was wary. He still wasn't getting through. 'You can have anything you want to make life easier. Think about it. Being married could work for all of us.'

'I see.'

'Do you?' She wasn't reacting how he'd hoped.

'We'd live here?'

'Of course.' He waited, his fingers tapping the counter. Then when he couldn't bear the silence any longer, 'You're not saying much.' Not what he'd expected from someone who was usually talkative and cheerful.

She stood up abruptly. 'I think you're testing me to see what I really want from you. You're wondering if I'm going to be like your ex. Well, news flash. I'm not. By the way, you left out any mention of a pre-nup, which I'm sure is part of the deal.'

What could he say? Behind his need to have Anastasia in his life lay the nagging worry he'd screwed up by not believing in her. He wanted to believe he'd laid that to rest, but here it was again, swinging in front of him.

'As far as proposals go, yours needs a lot of practice. I'm not marrying you just to share Holly. If I'm ever to marry, it will be for one reason only. Love.' She faltered and looked away.

'Anastasia—'

'My name is Stacey,' she hissed. 'Now, if you don't mind, I'll take Holly home. It's been a long day for her.

'And for me,' he thought she muttered as she pushed past him.

Noah watched as she stormed out of the room. He'd turned the day cold in the last few minutes. He'd got it all wrong. His heart ached for the missed chance of happiness. Instead of telling her his feelings, he'd gone about his offer like a business proposal and not a loving marriage one, not a declaration of love. Stacey would not give him an opportunity to redeem himself. Now that he'd blown it, he understood how much he wanted her in his life, at his side, as his wife. Because he did love her so much it was impossible to breathe properly any more.

* * *

'Here, have this seat.' A man stood up as Stacey entered the train carriage holding onto Holly and the stroller, with her heavy bag slung over her shoulder.

'Thank you so much.' She couldn't find the strength to argue, neither did she have enough energy to stand for the ride home. She didn't think she'd ever feel strong again after Noah had decimated her hopes so quickly and sharply. Sure, she could have said yes and married him. For what? There was no mention of love, and that's all she ever wanted from a relationship and marriage.

Love came with understanding, caring, sharing, support. Not a cool hope that they could live under the same roof while seeing their daughter had the life she deserved. Because there was no chance of that when Noah didn't love her. Holly was different. He genuinely loved her already. Like it had been for her when Holly was born, he'd fallen for his daughter quickly. But that wasn't a reason for her to accept his proposal.

Stacey hugged Holly. The last thing she was interested in was his money. It hurt that he might have thought so for one minute. She loved him beyond reason. Living with him, sharing a bed with him as his wife, would be unbearable since he obviously didn't have the same feelings for her. At least she knew where she stood. On the outside. Alone with her love.

She gave a cynical huff. When it came to men she never got it right. She'd loved Angus and look where that had got her. Now she loved another man who only wanted her to stay around for all the wrong reasons. Angus had been right about one thing: their love did lack the passion he'd found with his new partner, and which she'd discovered with Noah. Noah was wrong to think they could be together long term with only passion and not love to live by.

Holding Holly tight, she watched the passing roads and buildings without seeing them. Now what? She worked with Noah, had to face him every day. Had to figure out how to share their daughter without becoming angry or hurt every time she handed Holly over.

Her stop came far too quickly. She wasn't ready to go home. One look and her parents would know what had happened. With Holly in the stroller she headed out of the station and down the road in the opposite direction of home.

'Damn you, Noah Kennedy. Why couldn't you be an ordinary guy who didn't make me feel vulnerable? Didn't steal my heart? Why did you have to return to London, and the hospital where I work? What was wrong with any of the other hospitals in the city? Or even staying in Auckland?'

She bumped into a woman and received a glare.

'Sorry,' Stacey muttered, aware she hadn't been looking where she was going. She was outside a café buzzing with people. An open fire tempted her in out of the chilly air, and she found an empty table at the back of the café. After ordering herself coffee and a biscuit for Holly, she sat down and stared at her clasped hands. This was her fault for thinking Noah might return her feelings. Once again she'd been naïve. They'd had great sex one night three years ago, and had then repeated it since finding each other again. Not a lot to go falling in love on. But people did fall quickly. She'd read about it often. Seen it with her close friends.

Noah's life was the polar opposite of hers. He was wealthy, she barely made ends meet. They both cared about people and looked after them. She had a close family, he didn't. His aunt and uncle were cold, and from what he'd told her nothing like his parents had been. Obviously he still missed them a lot. His wife had hurt him, hadn't delivered on what he'd required from a marriage.

She could. She would. But she wasn't marrying him if he didn't love her.

Deep in her bag the phone rang. Not wanting to talk to anyone, Stacey ignored it.

But she couldn't keep Holly out for ever. Finally she trudged home, pushing the stroller and wishing she hadn't got out of bed that morning.

CHAPTER TEN

THE NEXT MORNING Noah parked outside the Wainwright house and drew a deep breath. Then he climbed out of his four-wheel drive and headed up the path to the front door to knock loudly.

When the door swung open, it took all his willpower not to pull Stacey into his arms and never let go. To beg her for another chance. She looked sad, and dark shadows under her eyes suggested she'd had as little sleep as he had. He'd done that to her. 'I'm really sorry.'

She blinked. Then nodded. 'Okay.'

When she made to shut the door, he stepped forward. 'Wait. I need to talk to you.'

The door stopped moving. 'I think you said it all yesterday, Noah. Quite bluntly, in fact.'

'I haven't come here to make demands.'

'I'm sure you haven't. But you will anyway.' Again the door was being pushed closed.

'Stacey, give me five minutes and if, after

that, you tell me to go, I will.' Five hours wouldn't be anywhere long enough to say what was in his head. In his heart. But how else could he get her to listen to him? Going down on bended knee might work, but Stacey would more likely laugh at him.

'Why, Noah? We are so different it'd be funny if not for Holly.'

'No, we're not. We laugh at the same things. We have the same values. And, yes, we have Holly.'

'Holly can't be used to get me back on side.'

Stacey was strong and self-contained. She fought for what she believed in. He'd found the woman he'd been searching for most of his life. She was absolutely nothing like Christine in any way, shape or form. Now he had to convince her to give him a chance. The way she was looking at him with impatience in her expression said it wasn't going to be easy.

'You're right. And I had no intention of using her to get you to listen to me.' He waited, aware that anything else he said might close the door firmly in his face.

Finally Stacey stepped back and held the door wide.

He stepped inside before she could change her mind.

When the latch on the door snapped shut the

air around them felt a little warmer, and the tension in his body eased a little. He was nowhere near reaching what he'd set out for when he'd driven off from home, but Stacey was prepared to hear him out. All in five minutes.

With Toby present. His stomach clenched when he saw Stacey's brother seated at the table with Holly on his knee as they ate breakfast. No sign of her parents. Then he recalled Stacey saying something about them being away for the weekend. Of course he'd known the chances of being alone with Stacey were still remote, but he'd hoped for a miracle, and it hadn't been forthcoming.

'Morning, Toby. Hello, Holly.' Noah brushed a hand over her sweet head and felt his heart lurch. She was gorgeous. She was his and Stacey's. More Stacey's than his. So far she'd done all the parenting. Done it well, and with love.

'Hi, Noah. You're out early. I hope you've come to put a smile on Sis's face. She's been in a grump for ever.'

'Shut up, Toby,' Stacey snapped as she filled the kettle.

Her brother merely shrugged. 'See what I mean?'

'Haven't you got somewhere to be?' Stacey glared at him.

Toby grinned. 'Yep. Holly and I are going to the park to play football, aren't we, Hols?'

'Yes, football!'

Stacey looked flustered. 'No, leave Holly here.'

Did she need to have her girl by her side while he was here? Noah wondered.

'I want football,' Holly demanded.

Getting more like her mother every day. 'I won't be long,' Noah said. Though he hoped that wasn't the case. 'I'm sure Holly will love getting outside.'

'Yeah, sis, we'll be back soon. We need to make the most of the fine day.'

Stacey's shoulders slumped. 'Go on, then. I'll join you shortly.' Then she looked directly at Noah. 'This had better be good.'

Noah waited while Toby got Holly into a thick jacket and slipped her tiny feet into pink shoes and tied the laces firmly, all the while watching his daughter and loving her, and trying not to glance at Stacey for fear of seeing anguish in those beautiful eyes. For she'd think he was here to lay down the rules on how they raised Holly. Little did she know what he really wanted to tell her.

Finally they were gone and silence fell, broken only by the sound of coffee being poured from the plunger into mismatched mugs.

Stacey placed them on the table and sat down, then waited.

Five minutes. Would she really hold him to that? Then again, this was Stacey and he couldn't rely on her to be kind to him. Slowly he sank onto a chair opposite her. Where to start? During the long night he'd worked out how to approach her, and now it had all gone out the door with Holly and Toby. He hadn't a clue where to start. There was a lot to explain. But only one thing was really important. He gulped.

Sipped the steaming coffee. Looked at Stacey. His Anastasia. Her hands were gripping her mug, her gaze fixed on the table. Could he do this? He had to or lose out for ever. His heart thumped, his belly was in a knot. 'Stacey…' He paused, waiting for her to lift her head. When she didn't, he said, 'Please look at me.'

Slowly she obliged, wariness in her expression.

'Stacey, I love you.'

Her eyes widened, but the wariness remained.

Noah reached for her shaking hands and removed the mug before enfolding her fingers in his. 'I love you, everything about you. Your bravery, laughter, sense of worth and consideration for others, even the way you stand up to me. Your love for our daughter.'

Her fingers tightened under his, loosened. 'Is that what this is about? Holly?'

Her question didn't surprise him, and yet it still hurt. 'Not at all. I'm not making this up. I've probably loved you from the night we first met, only I tried to deny it, especially when we met up again a couple of weeks back. You gave me hope that I'd actually find someone I could be happy with, and love and be loved.'

Her hands turned over and she gripped him. 'Noah, are you sure? I don't want to hurt you. Neither do I want to find that you've changed your mind, and think you've got it all wrong.' She was looking at him with such longing the lump of fear that she might reject him out of self-preservation melted. 'I don't wish to be hurt by you either.'

Standing up, he rounded the table and pulled her up into his arms. 'I am more certain of my love for you than I am about anything else. I would never willingly hurt you. Will you marry me? As in a real marriage filled with love?'

Noah was asking her to marry him again. Twice in two days. Should she believe him? Or was this another way to get her to compromise on her own needs? Stacey's heart stopped as she gazed into his eyes. This time there was love in his gaze, his face, in the hands holding her.

No hesitation at all. He'd said he loved her before anything else.

She wanted to believe him with everything she had.

'Stacey, I made a mistake when I married last time. I thought I could change love, make it fit to suit. This time I know I've found love, and I don't want to alter anything. It's you who's stolen my heart. You're all I've been hoping for. I love you, Anastasia Stacey Wainwright.'

Relief and love bubbled up as her heart kickstarted and sent warmth racing through her chilled body. She clasped his hands. 'I've always loved you, Noah. Right from the moment you took my hand to lead me further onto the dance floor. Don't ask me how it happened so quickly, or so truly. I have no idea, except it's right. I love you, too.' Locking her eyes on his, she drew a breath and said in as firm a voice as the love bubbling through her allowed, 'Yes, I will marry you.'

Then she was being spun around in his arms as he yelled, 'I'm getting married.'

'So am I.' Stacey laughed, leaning closer to kiss him. It was a kiss that went on for ever and left her breathless—and so happy she had to pinch herself.

The coffee was cold when they finally sat down, this time side by side, her hand in Noah's.

'Who needs coffee anyway?' Noah grinned. 'I've got you.'

He loved her. He really did. It had been so easy to tell him she loved him. After a night of tears and anger and frustration over his blunt proposal yesterday, she'd accepted his love and offered hers in return. No questions, no doubts. She stared at this man who'd changed her life in so many ways. This would never have happened if he hadn't returned from Auckland.

'Stop overthinking it, Stacey. We will work through everything—together.' He paused and looked away, then back at her. 'I've spent my life looking for the kind of love my parents shared. I was always a part of that and to lose them meant I lost love as well. Then I met you. We danced and made love, then I went away. That night I felt a tingle of anticipation I'd not known before. Throughout those years I dreamt that you were with me, making love or dancing as we'd done that night.

'When we met again those feelings returned, stronger than ever. Yet I hesitated, wary of being hurt again, of being used for what I had and not who I am. Yesterday when I asked you to marry me I meant it, but I admit my doubts were exposing themselves, causing me to voice things I'd never intended to. I'm so sorry.'

Squeezing his hand, Stacey leaned in to brush

a kiss over his mouth. 'It's all right. We got there in the end.' She took her time with what she had to say. 'About your wealth. It isn't something I'm after. If anything, it frightens me a little. But I'm sure I'll manage.' She smiled. 'Seriously, it's more important that we're happy, and that Holly's happy and grows up knowing she's loved by her parents. And that we love each other.'

'We do. She will.' His look was fierce, and protective.

Stacey sighed with happiness. All was good, very good, and she'd found her man was on the same page as her. 'I love you, Noah Kennedy.' And she kissed him like they had all the time in the world. Which they did because they had found each other and would be together for ever.

* * * * *